INGRID WEAVER

Her Baby's Bodyguard

ROMANTIC
SUSPENSE

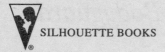 **SILHOUETTE BOOKS**

Recycling programs for this product may not exist in your area.

ISBN-13: 978-0-373-27674-5

HER BABY'S BODYGUARD

Visit Silhouette Books at www.eHarlequin.com

Printed in U.S.A.

Books by Ingrid Weaver

Silhouette Romantic Suspense

True Blue #570
True Lies #660
On the Way
  to a Wedding... #761
Engaging Sam #875
What the Baby Knew #939
Cinderella's Secret
  Agent #1076
Fugitive Hearts #1101
Under the King's Command #1184
★*Eye of the Beholder* #1204
★*Seven Days to Forever* #1216
★*Aim for the Heart* #1258
In Destiny's Shadow #1329
†*The Angel and the Outlaw* #1352
†*Loving the Lone Wolf* #1369
†*Romancing the Renegade* #1389
★★*Her Baby's Bodyguard* #1604

★Eagle Squadron
†Payback
★★Eagle Squadron: Countdown

Silhouette
Special Edition

The Wolf and the
Woman's Touch #1056

Silhouette Books

Family Secrets
 "The Insider"

INGRID WEAVER

is a *USA TODAY* bestselling author of more than twenty-five books and has been published by Silhouette Books, Harlequin Books and Berkley/Jove. She is the recipient of a Romance Writers of America RITA® Award for Romantic Suspense and an *RT Book Reviews* Career Achievement Award. Currently she lives on a farm near Frankford, Ontario, where she grows organic veggies and Darwinian flowers in a neglected garden of tough love. She loves to hear from readers. You can visit her Web site at www.ingridweaver.com.

This book is dedicated to all the fans of
Eagle Squadron who asked for Jack's story.
He owes you his life.

Chapter 1

The crust of ice on the puddle cracked beneath Eva's boots, signaling her presence as clearly as a gunshot. She risked a glance over her shoulder. The road was still empty, yet how long would that last? The stitch in her side was getting worse. So was the cold. It would likely snow by morning. She clenched her teeth to silence their chattering and increased her pace.

The trees gave way to a cluster of buildings, but there should be no one here who would raise an alarm. The village had been deserted long before the complex had been constructed in the neighboring valley. Eva didn't know where the original inhabitants had gone—she'd never thought to ask—but they'd been too practical to leave much behind. What hadn't rotted had been carted away years ago. The sole traffic this road saw now was the monthly supply trucks that lumbered through without stopping. Only the village church had remained more or less intact, and that was because it had been built out of stone.

Katya stirred against her chest, no doubt jostled into wakefulness by Eva's quickened stride. Without pausing, Eva lowered the zipper on her coat and reached inside to adjust the sling she'd fashioned for the baby. It held Katya securely enough, but the knots were digging into Eva's neck and the small of her back. "Shh. Almost there, kitten," she whispered. She rubbed her palm over the baby's back. "It won't be long now. I promise."

Reassured by her touch, Katya burrowed closer to her mother's warmth. Within seconds, her body relaxed once more into sleep. Eva left her hand where it was, letting her fingers ride the rise and fall of her daughter's breathing. She needed the contact as much as Katya did.

The moon inched past a break in the clouds, turning Eva's breath white and spreading silver-blue over the rise where the church stood. Shadows of grave markers tilted among weed stalks that sparkled with frost. A birch tree grew at the edge of the churchyard, its bare branches swaying in the wind. Apart from that, nothing moved.

Was she too early? She'd lost track of time. It seemed as if an eternity had passed since she'd slipped past the guards at the west gate, but it was more likely less than an hour. Eva risked another glance behind her.

Even with six kilometers of pine forest and a ridge of limestone between her and the complex, the glow of its perimeter lights was visible against the sky. She had once liked the security the floodlights provided. Against the empty blackness of the surrounding, tree-shrouded slopes, it had been comforting. Eventually she'd grown to understand that the security measures had been for control, not protection. Burian enjoyed demonstrating his power over all within his range.

Not me. And not my daughter.

She sucked more air into her aching lungs, fastened her coat and headed for the stone church.

This was it. The point of no return. If there was a bridge through the valley she'd just crossed instead of a puddle-strewn road, it would be burning. Shouldn't she be feeling some sadness or at the very least regret? She was leaving her home, her country, turning her back on everything familiar.

But then, the complex had never felt like home. It had been where she worked, that was all. A place for her mind, not her heart. How long had it been since she'd allowed herself to yearn for more? For Katya's sake, she did now. Home should be sunshine and apple trees, the smell of bread cooling on a windowsill, the liquid, joyous trill of Grandma's canaries and the soft warmth of her mother's arms....

The road blurred. Eva blinked against the wind to clear her vision and stepped into the churchyard. The home of her memories was long gone, but she would make a new one. Just her and Katya. When she got to America, maybe she would look for a place with apple trees. They would be beautiful in the spring. She could lift Katya up to sniff the blossoms—

A shadow detached itself from one of the grave markers as Eva passed. It happened so swiftly that she had no chance to react. Before any sound could leave her throat, a man stepped behind her and clamped his large, gloved hand over her mouth.

Panic overrode her logic. If she'd stopped to think, she would have realized who would know she was coming. But she was tired and scared and struggled anyway.

Wrapping her arms around Katya, she kicked backward until her boot connected with the man's shin.

"Whoa, relax, Dr. Petrova." He eased the pressure on her mouth. "We're here to help you."

It was a man's voice, pitched low, closer to a whisper than to speech. He knew her name. And he was speaking English. That last fact penetrated her fear. She stilled.

"Our code word is eagle," he said. His tone was gentle, at odds with the strength in his grip. A trace of the American South flavored his words. "They told you that, didn't they?"

Another shard of panic dropped away. She nodded against his glove, then reached for his arm. Despite the thick coat he wore, it felt like steel. She tugged anyway.

"Sorry about startling you, but we couldn't let you scream." He lifted his hand from her mouth. "Are you all right?"

She nodded.

"Hate to ask, Dr. Petrova, because it seems pretty obvious to me who you are, but the brass are sticklers for details. Can you give me your code word?"

Her first attempt came out as a gasp. She had to swallow a few times before her voice worked. "Hatchling. My word is hatchling."

"Check. I've got her, guys."

Though he hadn't raised his voice, more shadows emerged from among the gravestones. No, not shadows but men. They were dressed in the kind of drab, shapeless winter coats the locals wore, and each held a rifle to his shoulder. They moved in silence in spite of the brittle weed stalks that covered the churchyard. None looked her way. Their attention was focused on the road and the forest at the edge of the village.

Help had really come. Oh, God. After so many weeks of waiting and worrying, it was truly happening. The wave of relief was almost as strong as her earlier panic had been. Eva realized she was trembling.

"Any problems getting here?"

She locked her knees to keep them steady and shook her head.

"Do you have the disk?"

She dipped her chin in a quick affirmative.

"You might as well give it to me for safekeeping, Dr. Petrova."

She turned to face him. Like the other men, he held a gun, but he had the barrel pointed toward the ground. He was tall—the top of her head barely reached his chin. A thick wool cap was pulled low over his ears, and the moon was behind him, so she couldn't see much of his features except for the outline of his jaw. It was square and tautly set. As were his shoulders. Although his black coat looked bulky, he didn't. Even motionless, he exuded an impression of lean strength. He stood with the readiness of a runner waiting for the starting pistol. Or a wolf stalking a deer.

Another tickle of fear fought with her logic. She breathed deeply a few times, forcing herself to think. Regardless of how gently this man had been speaking to her, she couldn't afford to trust him entirely. Too much was at stake. She lifted her chin, regretting her earlier display of weakness. "Thank you, but the disk is quite safe where it is." She kept her voice at a whisper, hoping he wouldn't detect the tremor in it. "I'll turn it over to the appropriate authorities once I am in American jurisdiction. No offense meant."

It was hard to tell for certain with his face in a shadow,

but he appeared to smile. "None taken," he replied. "They did say you were smart."

By this time, the other men had withdrawn to the edge of the road. From the woods on the far side of the church came the rumble of an engine. Eva jerked in alarm.

"It's okay, ma'am." The man gripped her elbow and steered her toward the noise. "That would be our ride."

A truck pulled onto the road. It was the same size as the supply trucks that went to the complex, but there the resemblance ended. Except for short metal panels that formed the sides, the rear part of the truck was covered with canvas. The rest of it was so rusty that there was nothing to reflect the moonlight except the windshield. It looked like a relic from a past war, held together with bits of wire and luck, not an uncommon sight in this region of the Caucasus.

Eva looked around. These men had probably chosen the truck so it wouldn't attract attention, but they didn't expect to make it all the way to the coast of the Black Sea in that, did they? "I was told we'd be going by helicopter."

"It'll be at our rendezvous point. This area is too hot to risk a landing, and we figured you would already have had enough of a stroll for one night." He guided her closer to the truck. "By the way, are you wearing a pack under your coat?"

Her hand automatically went to the bulge where Katya nestled. "I was instructed to bring no luggage, and I brought none."

"Uh-huh. That doesn't mean much. I've known a lot of ladies who see fit to pack a purse as big as a suitcase for a trip to the corner store. Is that what you have there?"

"I understand what's at stake better than anyone, and I made sure to raise no suspicions. I was very careful with my preparations. It will likely be more than twenty-four hours before anyone realizes I have left the complex, Mr....?"

"Norton. Sergeant Jack Norton."

Sergeant. Of course. She should have guessed the American government would send military people, but her contact had given only the barest details of the extraction plan.

Then again, she hadn't told her contact all the details, either.

One of the other men jumped to the truck's tailgate and pulled back a corner of the canvas tarp. A cloud of exhaust obscured Eva's view for a moment. When it cleared, she could see a faint, green light glowed from inside where a large man knelt in front of what appeared to be electronic equipment.

Still gripping her elbow, the sergeant tilted his head to regard her as they walked. "Nah, it's too big for a purse. Pardon the personal question, ma'am, but are you pregnant?"

"No, Sergeant Norton."

"Because if you are, you should let us know. The trip out could get rough. We want to be prepared if there could be any medical complications."

"I am not pregnant, I assure you. I'm in perfect health and don't expect you to make any allowances for me."

"Okay, great. So what are you hiding under that coat?"

She'd known they would find out sooner or later. Katya would need to be fed in another few hours. Eva had hoped to be safely on her way out of the country before that happened, but she could see that the soldier wasn't going to let this go. She splayed her fingers over the curve of Katya's back. "My daughter."

They were less than two meters from the back of the truck. He stopped dead and pulled her to a halt beside him. "Whoa. I couldn't have heard you right."

"You did. It shouldn't make any difference. She's almost three months old, so she'll be no trouble."

"You brought a *baby?*"

"Surely you don't expect I would leave her behind."

Because he was turned toward the moonlight, she could make out more of his features. His mouth was bracketed by twin lines that would probably crinkle into dimples when he smiled. Actually, he looked like a man to whom smiling came naturally. Laugh lines softened the corners of his eyes, but there was no trace of humor in his expression now. His lips were pressed thin and his eyes narrowed. A muscle twitched in the hollow of one cheek. "Dr. Petrova—"

"Shouldn't we be getting on the truck?"

For a large man, and one who spoke so gently, he could move surprisingly fast. He hitched the strap of his rifle over his shoulder, reached for the front of her coat and lowered the zipper.

Jack Norton had seen his share of trouble during his years with Eagle Squadron. He'd faced fanatics with bombs strapped to their bodies and enemy soldiers who were loaded up with enough weapons to fill an arsenal. He never took anything for granted. It was when a man felt safe that he usually bought it.

So he should have known this mission was going too smoothly.

It was a baby, all right. She was trussed up in a jury-rigged cloth carrier that held her across the woman's midriff like a combination apron and hammock. A lacy, knitted cap covered the baby's head. One tiny fist, wrapped in a mitten that trailed shiny ribbons, rested against her mouth. Luckily, her eyes were closed, which meant she was asleep, but how long that would last was anyone's guess.

Actually, it was up to Murphy, the guy who wrote the law about anything that could go wrong, would....

Jack looked more closely. The kid wasn't the only cargo the woman was hauling. Two lumpy cloth sacks dangled from strings on either side of the kiddy carrier. So, she hadn't lied—technically the sacks weren't luggage. The coat was large and knee-length, and she'd obviously made use of every square inch of space she had under there. It was a wonder she had been able to walk one klick like that let alone six.

Jack tapped the largest sack. "What's in these?"

"Diapers and baby clothes," Eva replied. She spoke fluent English with only a hint of an accent, which was to be expected. According to army intelligence, she'd spent the first few years of her life with her mother's family in upstate New York. She'd been nearly four when her Russian father had gained custody.

Eva brushed his hand away and zipped her coat closed. Not all the way, though. He could see that she'd left a gap at the top for air. "I don't want her to get cold," she continued. "She might wake up."

"Right. We sure wouldn't want that." His mind filled with crying-baby scenarios, none of them good. They were in hostile territory on a mission his government would disavow any knowledge of if it went wrong. Discretion was essential. That's why the major had made the team plan for every contingency.

Having an infant along wasn't one of them.

Eva stepped closer and poked her index finger at Jack's

chest. "I made a bargain with the American government, Sergeant Norton. Safety and asylum in exchange for my cooperation. I expect you to honor it."

He snapped his gaze to her face. Could she think they would leave her here?

One look in her eyes told him that she wasn't thinking at all. She was terrified. That's why she had concealed the kid and why she'd refused to part with the disk. Those shivers he'd felt through her arm probably weren't all due to the cold. She didn't trust him. His reaction to her excess cargo wasn't helping matters.

She'd taken him by surprise, that's all. But damn, a baby? Even when he wasn't on a mission, he kept as far away from those as he could.

Jack took her hand from his chest and gave it a squeeze. "You've got me confused with the politicians, Dr. Petrova. I'm a soldier. We take our honor seriously."

She didn't relax. Instead, her expression tightened further. It made her look more like the photograph that intel had provided.

Like the rest of the team, Jack had committed that picture to memory during their briefing. The shot had been more than ten years old, taken when she'd been awarded a doctoral degree in chemistry from Moscow University when she'd been nineteen. In it she'd looked far too serious for her age, as if she'd been trying to prove something. She'd stared unsmiling at the camera, a regular ice princess with her pale blue eyes and platinum hair. Her high cheekbones and delicate jaw hadn't changed since then, though her lips seemed fuller. He wondered briefly whether she still wore her hair long, yet nothing showed from under the thick cap that she wore.

But as he'd just discovered, winter clothes were good for hiding all sorts of things.

"The major sent the word, Norton. We're moving out."

He shifted his attention to the truck. Tyler Matheson stood in the center of the back opening, one hand on the canvas and the other on his weapon. He would be covering the rear as they moved. Tyler was Eagle Squadron's new ordnance specialist and was proving to be the best marksman the team had ever had in spite of his rookie status. Jack acknowledged Tyler's warning with a nod. "Be right there, junior."

Tyler hopped to the ground with the agility of the cowboy he used to be, then moved around the truck to the driver's door to exchange a few words with Kurt Lang. Sergeant Lang would be doing the driving on this mission, as he usually did whenever something on wheels was involved. The man had an affinity for machines, which would have been spooky if it hadn't kept proving so useful. Specialist Vic Gonzales would be riding shotgun beside Kurt once he finished his forward sweep of the area. They would pick him up on the way. Like Tyler, though, Gonzales would only open fire as a last resort. They were counting on intelligence to steer them away from trouble. To that end, Duncan Colbert, headphones clamped to his shaved head, knelt in front of the communication equipment he'd set up on the truck bed.

Quick and clean, that's how Eagle Squadron liked to operate. They were usually long gone before anyone realized they'd been there. The five members of the team who were taking part in this mission had run through the plan until they could have done it in their sleep. Every man knew his role in it, including Jack. As

Eagle Squadron's medic, he'd been put in charge of their passenger.

Make that passengers.

Jack was confident the other guys would do their jobs. It was up to him to play the hand he'd been dealt.

He firmed his grip on Eva and led her forward. "We'll try to keep you and your daughter comfortable," he said. "But it's going to be bumpy."

"Neither I nor my child will break, Sergeant Norton."

She was using a tone that would go with the ice princess picture, he thought. It was probably an attempt to distract him from the trembling in her fingers. "This will go easier if you remember we're on your side, Dr. Petrova. We're the good guys."

"You're soldiers."

"Same thing."

"You're only as good as the orders you follow."

What kind of men had she been around to have gained such a low opinion of them? "My orders are to get you and what you're carrying safely to American jurisdiction," Jack said. "I interpret that to mean *everything* you're carrying, not just the disk, so you've got nothing to worry about." He stopped at the back of the truck, took one look at the height of the tailgate and then leaned over to scoop Eva into his arms.

She gasped. "Sergeant!"

She was lighter than he'd expected, even with her extras. Instead of simply lifting her into the back and getting in after her, he carried her with him as he climbed inside.

Duncan looked up when the truck dipped with their weight. The moment he saw the bulge beneath Eva's coat, he pulled off his headphones. "Ma'am, are you pregnant?"

Jack spoke before she could answer. "Nope. Not anymore. Ma'am, this is Duncan Colbert."

She acknowledged the introduction with as much dignity as she could, considering her position.

Duncan frowned and looked at Jack. "What's that mean, not anymore?"

"Dr. Petrova brought her kid along." Jack picked his way through the loose bark that littered the rusty floor. Apparently, the truck he'd acquired had been last used for hauling firewood. He set Eva on her feet where the cargo bed met the truck cab. "Stay here, ma'am. It should be the most sheltered spot."

"I need no special treatment."

"Well, with Lang and Gonzales up front, the cab's going to be crowded, and you probably don't want to get too close to Matheson when he's armed, so this is the only spot left." He stuffed his gloves into his pocket and put down his gun so he could peel off his coat and spread it in front of her. "You can sit on this."

"Thank you, but as I said, I need no special—"

"There might be spiders in the bark."

She hesitated for less than a second before she sank to the cushion Jack's coat provided and wrapped her arms around her baby. Her lips trembled. She pressed them together and inhaled hard through her nose.

Jack amended his assessment of her mental state, adding exhausted to terrified. He had a crazy urge to sit beside her and pull her, baby and all, into his arms. She'd felt good there. But that would probably bring out the ice princess again. He took one of her hands and guided it toward a loop of strapping that hung from the truck's short side wall. "You might want to hold on to that once we start moving."

She nodded and threaded her fingers through the loop.

Tyler returned and climbed into the truck, pulled up the tailgate and dropped the canvas into place. He spoke without turning around. "I heard you talking through the canvas, doc. It sounded like you said she brought a kid. Tell me I heard wrong."

"Sorry, junior, you heard right. We have a baby on board." Jack glanced from Tyler to Duncan. "Hey, either of you wouldn't happen to have one of those signs to stick on the windshield, would you?"

Tyler grunted, donned a pair of night-vision goggles and swung his weapon to his shoulder to sight through the back opening. Duncan muttered something about Murphy and put his headphones back on.

Their lack of reaction didn't surprise Jack. They didn't have the luxury for anything else. He leaned past Eva to rap at the window to the cab. "Okay, Kurt. We're ready."

The truck jerked into motion. Eva knocked into the side of the truck with her shoulder. Still holding the strap, she shifted her position so she could draw up her knees and put her back to the low wall for support.

"Are you all right?" Jack asked.

"Yes, thank you."

"It won't be long now. If you need anything, let me know."

She opened her coat just enough to slip her hand inside. "We'll be fine."

He regarded her for a while to make sure she had steadied. Now that she was sitting, the sacks of baby clothes would be resting on the floor and her drawn up legs would take most of the baby's weight. She still looked exhausted, but some of that could be due to the green glow from Duncan's instruments. Jack went over to squat beside him. "What's the latest intel on the rendezvous site, Duncan?"

"Not good. Weather's coming in."

"Lang will get us there."

"We have to hope the bird can land. It could get messy." He tipped his head toward Eva. "Are you sure she's got a baby?"

"Saw her myself. She was asleep."

"My sister's boys used to sleep as long as they were moving. Especially on car rides. She told me they'd be out like a light as soon as she left the driveway. Sometimes she'd stuff them in their seats and take a drive around the block just to get some peace." He pressed the transmitter on his headphones. "Say again, Gonzales?"

The truck hit a bump, jolting Jack into the air. He glanced back at Eva to make sure she was still hanging on, then shoved aside a stray piece of wood and braced his knuckles against the floor. "What's going on, Duncan?"

"Gonzales spotted a patrol."

"How far away?"

"Less than a mile ahead."

Ahead? If there had been a pursuit, it should have come from behind. This was either bad luck or someone had guessed they were coming. The first possibility was just par for the course, but the latter could scuttle the mission before it got started. They could only hope that Eva had been as careful with her preparations as she'd claimed.

Duncan glanced at the map on the laptop and spoke into his transmitter. "Lang, we'll try to go around them.

There's a track coming up on the left about a hundred yards." He tensed and grabbed the equipment. "Sharp turn, everyone."

Jack dove for Eva and landed beside her just as the truck lurched to the left. He put his hand over hers to grip the packing strap, cushioning her from the impact as they slammed against the side. The truck slowed only long enough to allow Gonzales to jump into the cab, then began accelerating uphill even before the passenger door slammed. Bark and bits of wood slid backward. Jack dug the edge of one boot into a row of rivets in the floor, braced his legs and twisted to lock his free arm around Eva. "Hang on!"

Her face was mere inches from his, so he could clearly see the fear in her eyes. She didn't protest about his help this time. She would have heard Duncan as well as Jack had, and she was obviously bright enough to have understood the danger they were in.

A muffled wail rose from her coat. One tiny, mittened fist knocked against Jack's sleeve where his arm stretched across Eva's chest. Despite the rocking of the truck, she dipped her head toward the baby, caught the tiny fist in her hand and brought it to her lips. "Shh, kitten. Don't cry. I won't let anything hurt you. I promise."

The change in Eva's voice was startling. It was as tender as a kiss, completely unlike the brittle tones she'd been using with Jack. And in spite of her fear, the promise to her daughter hadn't sounded like idle words that had been spoken in order to comfort. The vow had vibrated with courage any soldier would understand.

She would need all the courage she could scrape up, Jack thought. In the next instant, something whizzed past their heads. Moonlight winked through a scattering of new holes in the truck's canvas side. Over the grumble of the engine and the crunching of tires on the rocky track came the staccato pops of automatic weapons.

So much for quick and clean. Murphy must be working overtime tonight. Jack pushed Eva to the floor and curled himself over both her and the baby.

Chapter 2

Pain seared through Eva's side. She fought to control it, forcing herself to inhale in short bursts, but her ribs stung with each heartbeat. If only the ground would stop moving, yet it kept bouncing and shifting beneath her. It smelled like wool and soap.

She blinked hard and concentrated on her surroundings instead of the pain. She was lying on her side on the floor of the truck. Sergeant Norton's coat was beneath her cheek. She could feel the pressure of his thighs at her back and the weight of his chest on her shoulder. With his hands braced in front of her and his knees behind her, he was caging her beneath his body because…because…

Her brain clicked back into gear. Oh, God! She could hear gunfire. Katya!

Before panic could take hold, she felt movement against her breasts. Katya was squirming in the confines of the cloth sling. Over the gunfire and the roar of the truck's engine Eva heard the baby's restless wails. She sounded cranky, not hurt. Thank God. If anything happened to this child because of her decision...

The thought was too terrible to consider. She dragged her arm around the baby, then pressed her nose to Katya's head, drawing strength from the familiar, powder-sweet scent of the baby's scalp. "There's my brave girl," she murmured. "Mommy's here. Everything's fine."

Either her one-armed embrace or the sound of her voice penetrated Katya's temper. The wails tapered off to weary sobs. Eva drew up her knees, curling her body around her child the same way Sergeant Norton was using his own body to shelter the two of them.

He had probably saved their lives when he'd knocked her over. And he was continuing to risk his own by shielding them. Who did that for complete strangers? What kind of man was he? She had seen he wasn't happy when he'd discovered Katya, yet he'd sounded almost amused when he'd relayed the information to his companions. His voice could be gentle, and he had laugh lines around his eyes and mouth, though she could feel nothing soft about the rest of him. With his size he would likely crush them if he wasn't strong enough to hold his weight on his arms.

The truck hit a rock, tossing her into the air. She collided with the sergeant's body before slamming back down on her side. She clenched her jaw to keep from crying out at another stinging jab of pain. She must have fallen on a piece of wood when the shooting had started. Or there could have been splinters in the bark that covered the truck bed. That must be why her side was still hurting. The bouncing was making it worse, but she didn't dare try to sit up. She had to protect Katya.

Had she made a mistake? If she'd stayed at the

complex, Katya would be sleeping peacefully in her crib. No one would be shooting at them. They would be safe.

No, she told herself. They wouldn't have been safe. Unless she kept going, no one would be. Their own lives weren't the only ones at stake. The information on the disk she carried could lead to the deaths of thousands, maybe hundreds of thousands. The moment she'd learned where her research was truly leading, she'd begun looking for ways to halt it. Making a deal with the American government had seemed like the best solution, but what if there had been another way?

Eva touched her lips to Katya's forehead. The decision had been made, so she couldn't allow herself any second thoughts. She could only pray this child wouldn't be made to pay for her mother's choice.

The truck lurched, then straightened and steadied, as if they had regained the road. As the noise lessened, Eva realized that she could no longer hear any shooting.

The pressure on her shoulder eased as Sergeant Norton straightened his arms, but he didn't move away yet. His voice came from just above her head. "What do you see out there, junior?"

"Not much except lots of dark," the man at the rear of the truck replied. "I'd say we lost them. There were three men, maybe four. Vehicle looked like a big sport utility, handled heavy so it's probably armored."

"Any damage?"

"It's hard to tell with this rust bucket, but there's nothing obvious. They had plenty of firepower but not much accuracy."

"I'm picking up some chatter." It was the bald man who spoke, Colbert, the one with the electronic equipment. "It sounds like we ran into a patrol from the research complex, not government troops. They'd be the only paramilitary in this sector. They thought we were smugglers."

"Then they weren't trying to hit us, only scare us off," the man at the tailgate said. Matheson was his name, Eva remembered. As before, he spoke without turning around. "That's why they broke off the chase. We wouldn't be their problem once we got out of their area."

"Hard to say what they would consider their area," Colbert said. "Intel warned us Ryazan's enforcing a no-drive zone that covers more territory every year."

"Well, technically, we are smugglers, Duncan," Sergeant Norton put in. "The only difference is our contraband came to us." He brought his head close to Eva's. His breath was warm on her ear. "Sorry about the excitement back there, Dr. Petrova. How are you doing?"

Unexpected tears sprang to her eyes at the kindness in his tone. She blinked them away, impatient with herself. This man may have saved their lives, yet regardless of his heroic actions, his motive for protecting them hadn't been personal. He was just following orders. His government wanted her almost as much as they wanted the disk she carried.

She couldn't afford to trust him. She knew better than to trust any man. "I am fine, thank you."

He was silent for a moment, then pushed himself off her and patted her shoulder. "Okay, then. And the baby?"

"She appears unhurt."

"Great. Let me help you sit up."

"I can manage. We need no special treatment."

"Dr. Petrova…"

"How much longer—" she grimaced as the truck swayed around a bend "—to the helicopter?"

"Hang on, I'll find out." He got to his feet, stepped over her legs and went to crouch beside the electronic equipment. "How's our timetable?"

"Tighter than I'd like," Colbert replied. "The detour cost us."

"Let me see that satellite shot."

While the men spoke, Eva turned her attention to the task of sitting up. The extra weight from Katya and her bundles of supplies made it more difficult than she'd expected. She groped for the strap that was attached to the side of the truck and used it to haul herself upright. The change in position helped clear her head, but it brought fresh stinging from her waist to her armpit. Though she was no longer being tossed into the air as violently, the road was far from smooth. She felt every rut and pothole. Adding to her discomfort, the wind seemed to have increased since they'd started out, causing the truck to shake with each gust.

Eva took a cleansing breath, closed her eyes to gather her strength and concentrated on breathing shallowly through her mouth, using the same method for mastering pain that had gotten her through childbirth. If she could endure that, she could endure anything, especially a splinter.

Yet what kind of splinter would hurt this much? Or could have penetrated her winter coat?

"What's wrong?"

She opened her eyes to find that Sergeant Norton had returned and was kneeling in front of her. Although her vision had adjusted to the darkness, she still couldn't see much more of him than his silhouette against the glow from the communication instruments. He looked large and hard, uncompromisingly male, and she had an insane impulse to lean into his chest and feel the shelter of his body once more.

Was she getting delirious? She reminded herself again not to take his concern personally. "How much longer before we reach the helicopter?" she demanded.

"A while yet," he replied vaguely. He moved closer. "Dr. Petrova, I know you said you were fine, but you don't look that well."

"I believe I fell on some wood, that's all."

"Hey, Duncan," he said over his shoulder. "Tell Kurt to ease up for a few minutes."

"No can do, Jack. Weather's getting uglier by the minute. We've got to hustle."

"No!" Eva said at the same time. "There is no need to slow down on my account."

He took a penlight from a pocket on the leg of his pants and clicked it on. "All right," he said easily. "In the meantime, how about letting me check over the baby? I bet you wouldn't argue with that."

He was right. Eva should have thought of that herself. She looked at Katya. The mittens she'd knitted for her had fallen off, as had the cap. Her wispy hair gleamed almost white in the flashlight's narrow beam, and her face was flushed from her fussing. The sudden light startled her to silence. She looked around restlessly until she spotted Eva's face and gave a gurgle of recognition.

Eva managed a shaky smile. "There's my brave girl," she whispered.

"You did a good job with that carrier you rigged up." Sergeant Norton pushed apart the edges of her coat as he spoke. "What did you use, anyway?"

"A sheet from my bed. I knew its absence wouldn't be detected. I did not want to raise suspicions by taking

Katya's stroller." She panted a few times. "If anyone notices we aren't in our quarters they'll assume we couldn't have gone far."

"That was good thinking. This carrier would have kept the kid as steady as a seat belt, anyway." He directed the light at Katya while he ran his free hand over her head and back in a cursory examination. "Did you use the sheet for these extra sacks of stuff, too?"

"Yes. For the same reason."

"They probably helped cushion her." He wedged the flashlight between his knees and leaned forward to peel Eva's coat off her shoulders. "Okay. Your turn."

She attempted to pull away, but with her back against the side of the truck there was nowhere to go. "You said you were only checking Katya."

"Hold still. I saw blood on one of those cloth sacks."

Her heart froze. "Oh, God. No."

"The blood must be yours, not the baby's," he said. "There's none on that sling except where it goes around your side." He pulled a folded knife from another pocket and flicked it open. Without any warning, he sliced through the strings that suspended the bundles of spare baby clothes.

She tried to bat his hand away. As she'd learned earlier, though, there was no budging him. "Stop. What are you doing? Katya needs those things."

"I have to get rid of your cargo so I can see where the blood's coming from."

"No, it's nothing. Just a splinter."

As if she hadn't spoken, he tossed the bundles aside. "Duncan," he said, raising his voice. "Come over here and hold the kid for me."

"Sorry, Jack," he said, his fingers flying over the keyboard of a laptop computer. "I'm kind of busy right now."

"Junior?"

The man at the tailgate shook his head without turning around. "Don't look at me. I don't know anything about babies."

"What's to know? Pretend she's a bomb."

"Nope. Bombs are more predictable."

Eva crooked one arm around Katya. "She'll be frightened without me. This isn't necessary."

Sergeant Norton frowned and looked at Eva. "I'm a medic. While I'm not a doctor, I have been trained in basic first aid." He closed the knife with a flick of his wrist that made him look more like a hoodlum than a doctor. "And I intend to assess your wound."

"No, I—"

"Ma'am, I understand you're scared and for some reason you don't want to admit that you're hurt, but you're going to have to trust me on this. You won't be any good to your baby if you pass out from blood loss."

She couldn't argue with that reasoning. Not that she was going to trust him, but for Katya's sake, she had to allow him to help her. That was the logical thing to do. And this was hardly the time to think of pride or modesty. Not with their survival at stake. Eva glanced past him at the other two men, but their attention appeared totally focused on their tasks. The window to the cab of the truck seemed too grimy to see through, even if the men in the front chose to look back. She pressed her lips together and gave a curt nod.

Sergeant Norton undid the knots that held the sling behind her neck and waist, then lifted Katya out. He supported the baby stiffly across both his palms for a moment, as if unsure what to do with her. Taking advantage of her sudden freedom, Katya began wriggling and kicking her feet. The nylon snowsuit she wore was slippery, causing him to juggle her awkwardly.

"Cup your hand under her head and lay her along your arm," Eva said, motioning toward him. "Like an American football player."

It took a few attempts for the sergeant to comprehend what she described. Finally, he managed to do as she instructed, tucking Katya's legs under the crook of his elbow so he could hold her with only one hand. The baby looked tiny against his body, yet she was apparently happy with her new position. She brought her thumb to her mouth and stopped squirming.

As soon as Eva reassured herself that Katya was being held securely, the strength she'd managed to summon began to ebb. Without the warmth of her daughter against her chest, there was nothing to distract her from the pain that radiated across her ribs. She inhaled hard, then started the pattern of shallow panting once more.

Keeping the baby cradled against his side with one arm, Sergeant Norton clamped the flashlight between his teeth. With his free hand he pinched the lower edge of Eva's sweater and pulled it upward.

Her blouse clung wetly to her skin. She bit her lip to keep from crying out as the fabric was peeled away. The stinging deepened. Something hot trickled down her side to the waistband of her pants.

He let the flashlight drop from his mouth. "This is getting to be a bad habit of yours, Dr. Petrova."

Eva exhaled on a hiss. "What?"

"You're trying to hide things under your coat again."

"Sergeant, I'm not—"

"Save your breath, ma'am," he said. His fingertips

were featherlight as he touched her side. "It wasn't any splinter that caused this wound. It was a bullet."

The storm blew in faster than any of Duncan's meteorological program models had predicted, and as luck would have it, they were driving straight into the thick of it. The packed dirt that served as the road had already disappeared beneath a layer of snow. It was falling so fast that Jack could barely see the tracks they'd left behind them. Kurt had reduced his speed to maintain control as the wind buffeted the truck, but they were no longer concerned about making the rendezvous. Until the storm let up, the chopper wouldn't be coming. The objective now was to find somewhere to wait it out.

Jack let the tarp fall back into place and glanced over his shoulder. Eva had her eyes closed and was leaning against the side of the truck, but he knew she wasn't sleeping because her hands were curled in a white-knuckled grip over the baby. At his insistence, she'd laid the kid on her lap instead of returning her to the bed-sheet carrier and strapping her back on. It was her only concession to the compress that Jack had taped over her ribs.

That woman was giving him one surprise after another. Jack couldn't think of a single female of his acquaintance who would have even dreamt of concealing a bullet wound—or would have been capable of trying. Most men wouldn't have endured it as stoically as Eva had. And to top it off, her main concern, once she'd learned she'd been shot, was to ensure that the bullet had missed her baby.

Damn, she was something.

Beside him, Tyler adjusted the canvas to minimize the amount of snow that curled in and resumed his watch through the gap that remained. In spite of the weather, he hadn't relaxed his vigilance. "How bad is it?" he asked.

Jack knew Tyler wasn't referring to the storm. Though the other men had concentrated on their own responsibilities while they'd left Jack to tend to Eva, they would be as concerned about her condition as he was. "The bullet only grazed her," he replied, keeping his voice low so she wouldn't overhear. "It lost most of its velocity when it passed through the side panel of the truck."

"So it's not serious?"

"No, it's minor. She was lucky. There was no penetration. Just a shallow gouge where it skimmed along her rib cage." Just? Sure, if he'd been talking about one of the guys, he'd laugh this one off. They referred to anything that didn't involve broken bones or major organs as a flesh wound, and Eva's was just a flesh wound. "It's ugly, but the bleeding was already slowing down. She'll need some plastic work once we get back if she doesn't want a scar."

"It must have stung like hell when she got hit."

"Yeah."

"She never said a word. Why do you figure that?"

It was a question Jack had already asked himself. He'd noticed that Eva had been in rough shape as soon as she'd sat up. Her sweater was black so he hadn't been able to see the blood on it right away, but she probably wouldn't have allowed him to touch her at all if he hadn't used the ruse about examining her kid first. Her defensiveness had begun long before she'd been injured. She'd been prickly from the moment he'd confirmed her identity. "She doesn't fully trust us," he replied. "My guess is she's worried that we'll take the disk and leave her behind."

"Smart woman," Tyler said. "She must have realized what the brass are really after. There's some heavy-duty stuff on that disk."

"Yeah, well, then it's a good thing we take our orders from Major Redinger. He doesn't have much use for politics."

"Wonder what he'll say when he finds out about the kid."

"Knowing the major, he'll probably add babies to the list of possible scenarios we have to cover when we train for the next mission."

Tyler grunted a laugh. "You could use the practice. You looked like you were getting ready to rush the kid through the Giants' front four."

"The football grip was Eva's idea. It worked, too. Want me to show it to you?"

"No, thanks. Give me a nice, safe bomb any day." He tipped his rifle to blow the snow off the scope. "So, what's your take on our lady? Is she going to slow us down?"

"Not if she can help it. From what I've seen, she's got enough willpower to walk from here to the Black Sea."

"She didn't seem to like you much, Jack. Guess that legendary bedside manner of yours must be slipping."

"You're still too young to understand women, son. If you were old enough to shave, you'd realize she was scared."

Tyler lifted his night-vision goggles so he could slide Jack a look. "She's got reason to be scared of you, doc. I've seen your handiwork, and I wouldn't want you anywhere near me with a med kit."

Jack let the comment pass, mostly because he agreed. He glanced back at Eva and saw that she was still sitting quietly. He'd cleaned and dressed the wound as well as he'd been able to in a moving vehicle. There wasn't anything more he could do to make her comfortable, and he doubted whether she'd let him anyway.

During his years in the service he'd seen far worse injuries than hers. He hadn't balked at doing whatever was needed to save his patient. The other men knew that nothing fazed him, yet the sight of Eva's wound had turned his stomach. It had seemed so...wrong.

The kind of violence he was accustomed to didn't belong in her world. She was too delicate, too feminine to be treated like the hardened soldiers he usually dealt with. She should be on a bed, not on a battlefield. Her skin had gleamed like satin in the glare from the flashlight. It had felt like satin, too. He'd smelled the blood immediately, but he'd also gotten a whiff of some kind of flowery perfume and the sweet musk of a female. Even while he'd done his best to focus on the gash the bullet had left, he couldn't help being aware of how close his hand had been to the curve of her breast.

Oh, yeah. A very ripe, full breast that strained the confines of her bra. And noticing it was, considering the circumstances, totally unprofessional and bordering on sick. He shouldn't even be thinking of her as a woman.

To the international diplomats, Eva Petrova would be considered the latest pawn in their ongoing game of one-upmanship. To his government, she would be viewed as a valuable asset and to the Russians she probably would be viewed as a traitor. Her fate, once the team got her out of here, would be anyone's guess. But until then, she was in Jack's charge. He should have found a way to keep her safe. He probably should have followed his instincts and pulled her into his arms before the shooting had started. To protect her, that is. Apart from administering first aid, that was the only reason he could justify touching her.

As much as he admired Eva's courage, he couldn't afford to let his personal feelings distract him from his duty. They were still a long way from safety. For everyone's sake, the mission had to remain his first priority. He would need to be prepared to do whatever was required of him to ensure its success.

Scowling, Jack returned his attention to the storm.

"You realize that once the people at the research complex notice one of their scientists is missing, the patrol we ran into is going to figure out we must have her," Tyler said. He had replaced his goggles and was sighting through the rear of the truck again. "And considering how loud that kid wailed, there's a possibility they'll know we have her baby, too."

Jack sat back on his haunches. "Yeah. They'll probably catch hell for letting us go."

"Plus they'll know what kind of vehicle we're driving and what direction we went."

"Not good."

"Nope.

"Eva said we'd have twenty-four hours."

"Better hope our lady's right. The way this storm is shaping up, we won't be getting an evac anytime soon."

Chapter 3

Eva had to lean against the door of the hut to close it against the force of the wind. In spite of the snow that puffed through cracks in the stone walls and the tin roof, she sensed an immediate improvement in the temperature. She carried Katya to the low-backed wooden bench that was near the hearth, grateful for the fire the men had managed to build. Though low-ceilinged and crude, this building would provide better shelter for the night than the canvas-roofed truck. The baby had awakened fully shortly after they'd stopped moving, and she was sounding more insistent by the second. Her wails had escalated to the point where they were drowning out the noise of the storm.

Eva winced, though not because of the racket Katya was making. As far as she was concerned, nothing her child could do would ever bother her. The wince wasn't due to her injury, either. Thanks to some kind of numbing salve that Sergeant Norton had applied, the pain from the bullet wound had subsided to a dull ache. The binding he'd wrapped around her midriff was keeping the edges of torn skin from rubbing against her clothes with each movement. Her current discomfort was from another source entirely.

She sat on the bench and shifted Katya to her lap, then positioned herself so that her back was toward the doorway. For the moment they were alone, since the men were outside gathering more firewood or exploring what they had referred to as the perimeter. Yet even without privacy, Eva wouldn't have been able to delay any longer. She parted the front of her coat, lifted her sweater and undid her blouse. As if sensing that help was within reach, Katya's fussing grew frantic. The moment Eva bared her nipple, the baby latched on with a vengeance.

"I'm sorry, kitten," Eva whispered, using her forefinger to press her swollen breast away from her daughter's nose. "I know you were hungry. I was in a hurry, too."

Katya gave her a look of reproach and curled one tiny fist over the edge of Eva's nursing bra. Her cheeks worked in and out as if it had been days since she'd last been fed rather than hours.

Eva sighed in relief as the pressure in her breast began to ease. They had been fleeing for their lives, shot at by Burian's guards and were now trapped by a storm in somebody's abandoned hut, yet all that mattered to this child was being warm and having a full stomach. Life was so simple for her. Was there anything more beautiful, more trusting, more perfectly innocent than a nursing baby?

Eva's eyes blurred yet again. How many times had that happened tonight? The tears had been close to the surface from the moment she'd left the complex. After years of taking pride in her intellect, lately she had been deluged with emotions. She understood why. It was because of Katya and the physiological changes of being a mother. Even if she never opened another book, never worked out another equation or published another paper, she could never regret this little miracle. "You're such a brave girl, sweetheart. We'll get there soon."

Unfortunately, Eva didn't have any idea where *there* would be, other than possibly a place with apple trees. All she'd focused on was getting away from where she'd been. That was as far ahead as she'd been able to plan. It wasn't like her. For the past ten years, every step of her life had been mapped out beforehand. She made lists. She stuck to schedules. She thrived on routine and predictability. Now she didn't even know where she was.

While Katya continued to nurse with gusto, Eva looked around the room. The fire was warming the air, driving away the mustiness and the smell of disuse. This building appeared to have been abandoned far more recently than the ones in the village nearest to the complex. The glass in the windows was still intact, and there had been some oil left in the lamp that burned on the wooden table. On the opposite side of the room from the hearth there were two low platforms that had likely held mattresses. The owners had left most of their furniture, as if they had hoped to return.

Or as if they hadn't had the chance to take more than the essentials when they'd been forced to flee.

Could the influence of the complex have extended this far? Eva hoped not. But as she'd recently discovered, she'd been ignorant of many facets of the place's true operation. How could she have been such an idiot?

The answer was obvious. She had only herself to blame for her ignorance. She'd seen what she'd wanted to see and had rationalized away the rest. When Burian Ryazan had offered her the position on his research team, his timing couldn't have been better. She'd been feeling adrift, and Burian had made her feel wanted, perhaps a little dazzled. She had read all of his books even before she'd enrolled in his course at the university, so the fact that her professor had remembered her had surprised and pleased her. She had accepted without hesitation.

It had been like a fantasy come true, or even better, since she wouldn't have dared to hope for anything so perfect. A life of the mind, far from the distractions of the everyday world. Days filled with work that she loved and the mental stimulation of the most brilliant scientists in the country. The isolation of the new facility hadn't bothered her, nor had the tight control that had been kept on everyone's movements. She'd loved the clean spaciousness of the grounds and the sense of being part of something important, perhaps even historic, that would benefit mankind.

Yes, she truly had been a fool.

"You're what's perfect, kitten," she whispered, stroking her daughter's cheek. Katya paused and looked up sleepily. Eva lifted her to her shoulder and rubbed her back to help get rid of her air bubbles, then switched her to the other breast. Katya immediately curled her fingers into the strip of tape that held the compress in place.

Wincing, Eva reached for Katya's hand just as the door swung open behind her.

"What did you do? The kid's finally quiet."

Eva recognized the voice. "All babies cry, Sergeant Norton." She guided Katya's hand away from the bandage. "That's one way they communicate."

He closed the door, stamped his feet and walked past her to the fireplace. "Reminds me of a drill sergeant I once knew," he said. His arms were filled with the bundles that he'd taken from her on the truck. He dropped them on the floor near the hearth. "He had a good set of lungs, too."

Eva tried to tug the edge of her coat forward, but it was wedged tight beneath Katya's back. She pulled her sweater down to cover as much of her breast as she could.

"I'm glad the kid's sleeping," he went on, yanking off his gloves as he turned toward her. "That'll give me a chance to..." His words trailed off. "Whoa," he muttered.

"She isn't sleeping," Eva said, although she was stating the obvious. Sergeant Norton was standing directly in front of her, so he could clearly see what Katya was doing.

He cleared his throat, then focused on her side as he stuffed his gloves into his coat pockets. "I wanted to check your bandage," he said, drawing off his hat. "But I can see from here there's no fresh blood."

She told herself not to be embarrassed. He was only doing his job. He'd seen more skin when he'd tended to her injury on the truck, and between her sweater and Katya's head, her breast was mostly concealed. This was a perfectly natural function, and she wasn't about to cut short her child's feeding because of some misplaced modesty. "I will let you know when we're done, Sergeant Norton."

He lifted his gaze to hers. "I'm sorry, ma'am. I didn't mean to intrude."

"Yes, I realize that. It was unavoidable."

"How's your wound feeling? Any pain?"

"No."

"Would you tell me if there was?"

"I don't want to be a burden."

"It's not you that's holding us up. It's the storm."

"It's early in the season for this much snow, even at this elevation," she said. "It should stop soon."

"That would be good."

"Then we will be able to reach the helicopter."

"That's the plan."

She nodded, determined to maintain eye contact with him, although it wasn't easy. The fire and the oil lamp were providing more illumination than the moonlight in the churchyard had, and she hadn't been able to see much more than his silhouette in the truck, so this was the first time she was getting a good look at his face.

She hadn't realized how handsome he was. His hair was the color of sable, touched with gold from the firelight. Though it was cut short, it was too unruly to lay flat. It curled in soft waves that made her fingers tingle with the urge to test their texture. His eyes were the indefinable, changeable color between green and brown and were framed by lashes as dark as his hair. The combination of his harsh features and his laugh lines gave him the air of a rebellious boy trapped behind the mask of a man.

Why had she thought that? There was nothing boyish about him. His shoulders were broad and square. His hips were narrow and his legs long. He stood with the same athletic grace she'd noticed when she'd first seen him, like a predator watching his prey.

It wasn't fear that tickled through her this time. It was the instinctive, sexual awareness of a woman who was in the proximity of a very virile man.

God, no! She couldn't possibly think about Sergeant

Norton in that way. This awareness was merely a product of the circumstances, a side effect of being in danger and the adrenaline that it produced. Added to that was the intimacy of breast-feeding her child. She'd never done this in front of anyone before, let alone a man. A man whose touch she'd already felt on her body.

No. It meant nothing. She had to ignore it.

The fire crackled. The wind howled. Aside from that, the only sound in the hut was Katya's steady suckling. Which only heightened Eva's consciousness of their situation. She searched for something to say that would break the silence, even if it was another inane comment about the weather. "What is this place?" she asked.

"Place?"

"We couldn't have gone far enough to reach another village."

"From the looks of it, this was a farm. There's another building out back that was probably used to keep animals. That's junior's take on it, anyway. He says it looks like they had sheep." He wiped his forehead as if he was too hot, then shrugged off his coat. "He and Lang are storing the truck in there. They'll be coming in soon. Duncan and Gonzo drew first watch, so they'll let us know if we get company."

Eva watched him as he hung his coat over the back of one of the chairs that were ranged along the table. He appeared as uncomfortable with their situation as she was. At least the other men were still outside. She guessed by the way they had scattered upon their arrival here that the task of keeping track of her had fallen to Sergeant Norton. "Do you and the others usually work as a team?" she asked.

He dragged another chair closer to the fire, turned it

around and straddled the seat. He focused on the door. "That's right. We're from Eagle Squadron."

"Eagle Squadron," she repeated. "That explains the code words I was given for our rendezvous."

"Yeah, we like to keep things simple."

"Am I correct to assume you must be part of the Special Operations unit they call Delta Force?"

"Why would you think that?"

"Your government would want the mission kept secret. We have the same kind of elite soldiers in Russia."

"Russian commandos aren't in the same league as us, Dr. Petrova. Eagle Squadron's the best there is."

He delivered the boast as if it were fact. She felt her lips quirk before she realized that for all their sakes, she'd better hope the boast was accurate. "You appear to have worked together for some time."

"Lang and Gonzales have been with the team more than ten years, like me. Sergeant Colbert came on board around five years ago, after our intel specialist decided to have kids."

"Aren't you allowed to have families?"

"Sure, she just didn't want to go out in the field anymore."

"She? I didn't know women are permitted to join the Special Forces."

"Captain Fox wasn't officially on the team. We kind of borrowed her from Intelligence."

"I see," she said, although she didn't. "What about the big blond man you call junior?"

"That's Sergeant Matheson, our ordnance guy. The man he's replacing decided to go freelance and start up his own security contracting company. Junior's been with us for less than a year, but he's already proving himself to be one of the best soldiers I've worked with." He darted a glance at her. "But don't tell him I said that. Rookies need to be kept humble."

The trace of humor in his voice tempted her to relax, but she reminded herself not to let down her guard. "I hope this mission won't require him to prove his expertise."

"Don't worry, Dr. Petrova. You and your daughter are under our protection now. We won't let anything happen to either of you."

He sounded sincere, yet she still suspected his real orders were to protect the disk that she'd brought. She looked at the bundles he'd dropped near the hearth and wondered if he or one of his colleagues had searched them before he'd brought them inside. They seemed intact, but that didn't mean someone hadn't felt them from the outside.

He followed her gaze. "You said you were careful not to raise anyone's suspicions before you left."

"That's right."

"And that it could be a day before anyone misses you."

"Perhaps more."

"I don't understand that. Won't you be expected to work?"

"I scheduled a few days in my quarters to catch up on my reading, which isn't unusual for me. It's unlikely anyone would have a reason to disturb me."

"Wouldn't they expect to see you around the complex?"

"No. I often fix my meals myself rather than go to the main cafeteria, especially when I'm immersed in a project. I was moved to a self-contained apartment after Katya's birth so that her crying wouldn't disturb my neighbors. The walls are well insulated, so no one would be able to hear whether or not we were inside."

"Are there a lot of kids at the complex?"

"The facility is like a small university campus. It wasn't designed with children in mind, although there are a few. Many of the researchers bring their spouses, but not many bring babies. They prefer to send their children to boarding schools when they're old enough, because of the isolation."

"What do you do with your baby when you work?"

"I bring her to my office with me. There is no organized day care, so no one will remark on her absence tomorrow."

He got up to add a few sticks to the fire, then remained there and watched the flames. "What about her father?"

"He has his own responsibilities. He seldom has the time to see Katya."

"So he lives at the complex?"

"Yes."

"Is he a scientist, too?"

"Yes." It wasn't really a lie but only part of the truth.

"Won't he notice you're gone?"

"Not immediately. The research I do constitutes only one component of the overall project. My area of expertise is the theoretical side of biochemical engineering, such as mathematical modeling, so I work on a computer. That's why I can bring Katya to my office. Her father works in the lab, which is in a separate area of the complex."

"I meant, won't he miss you when you're not at work?"

"We no longer have a personal relationship. The last time I saw him was a few days ago at our regular staff meeting, but it's not uncommon for weeks to go by without any contact between us."

He appeared to digest that for a while. "And you didn't want to say goodbye to him?"

"No. I already assured you that I told no one. As I said, I know what's at stake, and it's not only our individual safety. Were you told what's on the disk I'm carrying?"

He poked at the fire with another stick. Flames flared from orange to yellow, highlighting the harsh planes of his face. "I heard you were developing a biological weapon. Some new kind of virus."

She tried to read his expression. She couldn't see any condemnation in it, yet how could she help but blame herself? "I regret more than you can imagine that my own work contributed to the Chameleon Virus program. I had believed we would unlock the secrets of prolonging human life, not destroying it. The very idea that I could have helped in the development of this...this evil is horrifying. The world has to learn the truth because only international pressure will ensure the research will be stopped."

There was more silence. When he spoke again, his voice was thoughtful. "I understand why you made the deal with our government, Dr. Petrova, and I respect that. It took a lot of guts to admit you were wrong and try to fix it." He tossed the stick into the fire. "But there's one thing about your actions I don't understand."

"Yes?"

He brushed off his hands on his pants and turned to face her squarely. "Why did you hide the fact that you were bringing a child?"

Her pulse jumped. "I didn't think it was relevant."

"Now I'm just a simple soldier, and I don't have the

education of you scientists or the smarts of the diplomats you made your deal with, but it's my guess you had to have a good reason for neglecting to mention your baby. I sure hope that reason doesn't come back to bite us."

Despite Sergeant Norton's disclaimer, Eva wasn't about to make the mistake of underestimating his intelligence. His questions were continuing to prove his perceptiveness. "I simply didn't want to be delayed by issues of child custody," she replied, giving another part-truth. "I couldn't predict how your people would have reacted."

"They'd still want your information. Once you're in the States, they'll get you a good lawyer."

"I was willing to offer myself as a pawn but not my daughter. Bureaucrats and courts don't always put the interests of the child first. I've seen how your justice system handles international custody cases, and I won't risk—" Her voice broke. She cleared her throat, annoyed that she'd once again shown weakness in front of this man. She cupped her hand over Katya's head. "She belongs with me."

Sergeant Norton pulled his chair forward until it was even with the bench where she was sitting. He straddled the chair once more, folding his arms over the back. "I read in your file that your mother was American and your father was Russian. You went to live with him after she died." He paused. "Is that why you're so worried about your daughter? Because of what happened to you?"

She should have realized that he would know her background. The American government would have investigated her thoroughly before agreeing to her deal. "What else did the file tell you?"

"It said your mother was a translator at the UN, and your father was a diplomat."

She moved her thumb over Katya's cheek. "They had very little in common. After their marriage dissolved, my mother and I went to live with my grandmother, and my father took a position in Bolivia. He didn't see me again until the day after my mother's funeral. He was a complete stranger to me, yet the court allowed him to take me from the only home and family that I'd known."

"That doesn't sound right."

"My father had many influential friends, including American politicians. My grandmother was just an ordinary woman and didn't have the resources to fight him in court."

He extended his arm to touch her knee. "I'm sorry. That must have been rough."

She shook her head. "Don't waste your sympathy on me. It's Katya I'm concerned about. I didn't want to deceive you about her, but I felt I had no choice."

"I can see why you thought that, after what happened to you, but your situation's different. You've got plenty of influential friends of your own in our government now. They wouldn't have scuttled your deal just because of a possible custody issue with one of your colleagues…" His words trailed off. "Katya's father's not just an ordinary scientist, is he? If he was, you wouldn't be so worried."

She'd realized he was perceptive. She hadn't anticipated to what extent. "It's not really relevant."

He gripped her knee and leaned closer. "I think it is, or you wouldn't be hiding it. Dr. Petrova, who is Katya's father?"

There was no hint of a smile around the edges of his eyes now, yet she glimpsed sympathy in the depths, a softness at odds with the determination that showed in his tightened jaw. His hold on her leg was firm, but his touch was still gentle. She wouldn't have expected that in a man of his size. It made her remember how carefully he'd cared for her wound and how tenderly his fingertips had skimmed over her bare skin.

At the thought, the sexual awareness that she'd thought she'd suppressed sprang back full force. He was leaning close enough for her to catch the scent of his body. It was the same clean tang of soap, wool and man that had clung to his coat. It enveloped her in a warmth that had nothing to do with the fire. She wanted him to touch her again. She wanted to feel the strength of his arms around her and the warmth of his breath on her ear....

All at once, she realized that she could no longer feel the tug of Katya at her breast. She glanced down. The baby's eyes were closed, and her jaw was slack with sleep. A drop of milk drizzled over her chin as she let Eva's nipple slide out of her mouth.

A blush seared Eva's skin from her cheeks to her chest. She'd wanted to use conversation to distract both Sergeant Norton and herself from this intimacy. It had worked too well. How could she have relaxed? How could she have forgotten, even for one second, that she was still sitting with her breast bared in front of a veritable stranger? She quickly shifted Katya's limp form to her shoulder, using her bent arm to cover herself. Only then did she risk a glance at Sergeant Norton's face.

He swallowed, then withdrew his hand and curled it over the back of his chair. His casual pose didn't change, yet she sensed a new tautness in the way he held his body.

She knew he couldn't have missed seeing her bare nipple. The fact hung in the silence between them. And the sexual awareness she should not—*must not*—feel strengthened until it was as tangible as the crackle of the flames on the hearth.

Eva lifted her chin. She wasn't going to allow herself to be uncomfortable over this. She hadn't been deliberately exposing herself. She certainly hadn't been trying to entice him. Under the circumstances, that would have been absurd.

Therefore, it was also absurd for her pulse to be accelerating. And for her blush to be deepening. She was no innocent young girl, she was a thirty-year-old woman, a mother. She had nothing to blush about. Above all, she certainly shouldn't be studying Jack's large, long-fingered hands and thinking about how before tonight it had been almost a year since she'd felt a man's touch.

She shouldn't be thinking of him as Jack either. He was Sergeant Norton.

The door swung open behind her to the sound of men's voices and the stamping of boots. Flames crackled and shot up the chimney as cold air swirled along the floor. In one swift motion, Sergeant Norton got to his feet and placed himself between her and the other men. "Hang on for a minute, Kurt," he said. "We're not done."

"Come on, Jack. You said you already slapped on a Band-Aid. What more do you need to do?"

"Do I tell you how to drive?"

"All the time."

While the men spoke, Eva laid Katya on her lap and hurried to fasten her bra and straighten her clothes, a task made more difficult because her hands were trembling. The sergeant was using his body to shield her and Katya again, only this time he wasn't trying to protect them from bullets. He was blocking them from the view of the other soldiers.

His gallantry only made her feel worse. He was

doing his best to act respectfully. She really shouldn't be thinking about his touch on her body.

"Leave the firewood by the door, junior."

"We'll need more before the night's over," Matheson said, moving toward the fireplace. "I haven't seen weather like this since I left Wyoming."

Sergeant Norton shot out his arm to stop him from going farther. "I said wait."

"It's all right," Eva said, settling Katya against her shoulder once more. She rose to her feet. "I'm finished."

Matheson shouldered Sergeant Norton's arm aside and deposited an armload of wood on the other side of the hearth from the bundles of Katya's supplies. He nodded a greeting to Eva, discarded his coat and went back to retrieve a pack he'd left near the door. Lang was already leaning over the table to set up the equipment that Colbert had been using in the truck. He gave Eva a quick smile before he bent to his work.

The hut had seemed small before, but with the arrival of two more of the men, the space shrank again. Like Sergeant Norton they were large and fit, and in a rough-edged way they could be considered handsome, as well. The men Eva was accustomed to exercised their minds far more than their bodies. Not that she thought for a moment these soldiers weren't intelligent. It's just that they were different from the intellectuals she worked with. More, well, virile. They were giving off male pheromones the way their coats were shedding snow.

And a minute ago, the handsomest of these soldiers had been looking at her naked breast.

No. She would *not* think about that. Or him. Holding Katya to her shoulder, Eva squeezed past Sergeant Norton and bent to retrieve one of her bundles.

"Hold on, Dr. Petrova," he said.

"I thought you already looked at my bandage."

"This isn't about your wound. It's about what you were saying before the guys came in."

She straightened. "I need to change Katya's diaper before I put her down for the night." She used the bundle she held to gesture toward the wooden platforms that stood beside the wall. "I'd like to use one of those bed frames. There aren't any mattresses, but my coat should be thick enough to provide padding for her."

He snagged her elbow before she could go by him. "I had asked you who Katya's father was."

"Yes, I remember you did."

"So, who is he?"

She could see that Sergeant Norton wasn't going to let the point go. From what he'd said earlier, he likely had guessed the answer. So why was she stalling? Perhaps part of the reason she hesitated was because she didn't want to acknowledge how big a mistake she had made. She'd been such a fool. And there was a very real possibility that her poor judgment could come back to bite them—just as the sergeant had said. "I had hoped we'd be on our way out of the country by now and there would be no need to mention this."

"Eva? We need to know what we're up against."

"I know." She pressed her cheek to Katya's head. "Her father is Burian Ryazan, the director of the complex."

Chapter 4

"Will you look at that? I don't know how the old girl got this far," Kurt Lang muttered, leaning under the hood of the truck. "Next time try stealing me a decent ride."

Jack directed the flashlight where Kurt was working. The shed was open on the south side, so they were spared the worst of the wind. Still, it was cold enough to numb his fingers. "Nah. I know how much you like a challenge."

"What's wrong, Kurt?" Tyler moved into the shed, using his hat to slap the snow off his coat. He stopped beside Jack to peer over the fender.

"For starters, the sparkplugs are covered in crud, and this air filter looks as if it took a mud bath."

"Maybe it did. The roads around here probably turn to soup when the ground thaws."

"And look at this slime." Kurt drew out the dipstick

and wiped it on a rag. "No one's changed the oil in this crate since the last ice age."

Jack knew that nothing irked Kurt more than a poorly maintained engine, just as nothing pleased him more than the chance to tinker with one. He turned to Tyler. "Has Duncan picked up any chatter on the radio, junior?"

"Nothing out of the ordinary," Tyler replied. "Base has been monitoring the cell traffic around the complex, too. They'd let us know if it sounded as if anyone noticed our lady is missing."

Jack wasn't reassured. In fact, he was getting increasingly restless. He looked past the truck to the strip of darkness that was visible at the front of the shed. There were only a few hours to go before sunrise. The snow was no longer falling, but the wind was whipping what was on the ground into stinging, horizontal sheets that limited the visibility to nil—not the best conditions for anyone wanting to travel a mountain road.

Chances were good that the patrol they'd run into the day before had holed up someplace because of the weather, too, yet for how long? Eva had claimed that no one would notice her absence for at least a day, but Jack found that hard to believe. Too many things could go wrong. He didn't know how the scientists at that place worked, but someone might decide they needed to ask Eva a question, or schedule a meeting or even hold a surprise fire drill. Maybe one of her neighbors would come over to borrow a cup of sugar. Any one of those scenarios could unravel her plan.

Still, he didn't think the alarm would have been raised yet, since she spent her nights alone. She hadn't told him that specifically, but that's what he figured since she did say no one would notice her bed sheets were gone, and she'd said she'd broken up with her baby's father.

If the man had been anyone else, the fact they were no longer an item would have been a good thing. But Burian Ryazan was no ordinary man. Intelligence had provided information on him, too. Ryazan was a brilliant, Nobel Prize-winning scientist who'd parlayed his distinguished looks and razor wit into pop-icon status in Russia. He'd been the guiding force behind establishing the fortified bioresearch complex in this next-to-inaccessible region of the Caucasus. He also had the political savvy to cultivate powerful allies, enough so that the complex got away with having its own little private army.

In short, Ryazan was smart, powerful and behaved like royalty. As ex-boyfriends went, they didn't get much worse. Eva was right to be worried.

The rest of the team hadn't been any happier than Jack when he'd broken the news to them. They'd known Ryazan would order a pursuit when he learned one of his scientists was missing. Things would go to a whole different level when he learned his child was gone, too.

This was going to get real personal, real fast.

Then again, it was already getting personal. As far as Jack was concerned, his own objectivity had gone up in smoke the instant he'd seen Eva nursing her baby.

Sure, he'd told himself not to look, but that wouldn't have helped. Even if they'd been in pitch darkness he would have heard the quiet swish of that baby drawing in milk, and he would have smelled the sweet, uniquely feminine scent that rose from Eva's bare skin. He'd have to have been dead to ignore all that.

What he couldn't understand was why it had affected him so powerfully. He'd seen plenty of breasts up close and personal, starting with Lise Thibault's in the backseat of her daddy's car when he'd been fifteen. Even though that particular encounter had ended embarrassingly quickly, he'd learned quickly, too. Getting there was half the fun, and there were countless creative ways to both give and take pleasure from a woman's breasts. Having a baby attached to one wasn't exactly provocative.

It should have been a major turnoff to see Eva's swollen, milky nipple. Yet it hadn't been. She was a woman, doing what a woman was made for. And he'd never been more conscious of being a man. Hell, his pulse was speeding up now just thinking about it.

Which was crazy. He'd spent his adult life avoiding entanglements that would lead to cozy little domestic scenes like the one he'd witnessed tonight. He steered away from women who were nesters. The women he dated knew full well he wasn't in it for the long run. They enjoyed what he gave them, which usually meant a good time and great sex.

Yet sharing those moments of intimacy with Eva had triggered an instinct that went deeper than the urge for sex. He'd felt a primitive, entirely male urge to protect, to possess, maybe even to belong....

Damn, this situation was messing with his mind. Sure he wanted to protect Eva and her baby. That was his job. And he already knew where he belonged. Right here, with his brothers in Eagle Squadron. He was physically attracted to Eva; it wasn't any more complicated than that. She was a good-looking woman, he was a healthy male and there were some sparks. So what? The fact remained that she was part of a mission, and that meant hands-off.

He'd meant what he'd told her when they'd met. He took his honor seriously.

Jack belatedly noticed that a man's shape had materialized from the darkness outside the barn. Where the hell had he come from? Jack automatically brought his rifle to his shoulder as he swung the flashlight toward the entrance.

"Stand down, doc," Gonzales said, holding up his palm as he walked into the flashlight's beam.

Jack lowered his gun fast. He had to keep his mind on business. If he hadn't been preoccupied with Eva, he would have sensed Gonzo approaching earlier—or at least recognized who it was. He glanced at Tyler.

To his credit, junior didn't comment on the fact that Jack had almost put a hole in one of their teammates. Kurt didn't say anything, either. He simply took the flashlight from him, propped it between the hood and the windshield so it shone on the engine and continued with his work.

Jack focused on the truck. The faster they completed this mission, the better it would be for all of them. He got antsy when he had to stay in one place for long, whether he was on a mission or on leave.

As if echoing his thoughts, Gonzales spoke. "Hate to break up this party you've got going out here, but Duncan's packing up his gizmos. Weather's due to lift in the next hour, so we've got to roll. Junior, it's your turn to scout ahead a few klicks."

The change in the air was immediate. Tyler pushed away from the fender and crammed his hat over his hair. Jack zipped up his coat, his pulse accelerating with the prospect of action this time, not because of thoughts of Eva.

Kurt pulled out the air filter and knocked it against the bumper. "Give me another half hour. I need to clean up the old girl some more or we won't get another mile."

"I'll tell Duncan we move out in thirty," Jack said, heading out of the shed with Tyler.

Gonzales looked at Jack. "You think you can get our cargo loaded by then?"

"No problem," he said. "I bet she'll be ready in twenty-eight."

"You'd lose that bet, Jack. Never knew a woman who didn't like to keep men waiting."

"Not Eva. If Lang's not ready, she'd probably start off without us."

"Twenty bucks says you're wrong," Gonzales said.

Jack snorted. "You already owe me thirty."

"Then make it fifty, and you'll owe me."

Tyler paused to turn up his collar. "You know the first thing the major told me when I joined the team, Gonzo?"

"Probably something about not spending all your time looking at yourself in a mirror like Duncan."

"Besides that," Tyler said.

"Not standing between Gonzo and a grilled steak?" Jack asked.

Tyler looked from one to the other. "I never heard about that. What happened?"

"I'm a man of strong appetites," Gonzales explained. "So what did Redinger tell you?"

"Never bet against Jack."

Jack punched Tyler in the arm as they moved outside. "Well, junior, there's hope for you yet."

Eva tried to run faster but couldn't seem to make her legs work. Grandma's farm was at the end of the road, past the hill with the red barn and the big silo. It was already dawn. The sun rose low and golden on the horizon, sending her shadow stretching like a giant ahead of her. What was she doing outside so early? She should be home in her own bed with the nursery-rhyme quilt and the stuffed horse with the floppy ear she liked to rub between her fingers. She must have gotten lost. If only she could get over the hill she would be able to see the orchard. She could find her way home then.

Yet her feet were too clumsy. The hilltop was getting farther, not nearer....

"Dr. Petrova?" Someone shook her shoulder. "Ma'am, you need to wake up."

Her eyelids felt too heavy to lift. She tried, because she wanted so badly to see over the hill....

"Ma'am, we're moving out."

The man's voice slid into her dream. She strained toward him. He would help her. She knew he would.

"I'm sorry," he said, squeezing her shoulder. His voice grew closer. She could feel his breath on her cheek. "I know you're tired, Eva, but you can go back to sleep when you get on the truck."

The sun, the shadow and the hill dissolved into the smell of wood smoke and the shuffling of booted feet.

For a few cowardly moments, Eva didn't want to move as she hung on to the last fragments of the dream. She hadn't had it in years, yet there had been a time—after she'd gone to live with her father—when it had come almost nightly. It had been her last connection to her home in a world that had turned suddenly alien. How many times had she screwed her eyes more tightly shut and tried to return to the dream because it had hurt too much to wake up?

But Grandma's orchard was gone. Everyone was gone. Eva had learned years ago that she wouldn't find them again no matter how fast she ran.

"Ma'am?"

Eva finally blinked her eyes open.

Sergeant Norton was leaning over her. Snow crystals shimmered from his hat and his coat. Beyond him, Colbert was using a stout stick to break up the embers that remained on the hearth. The only light came from the lamp that was on the table. The electronic equipment that had been there earlier was gone. So were the bundles of Katya's supplies.

"We only have a few minutes," the sergeant said.

Eva's pulse kicked as she came completely awake. Katya was still sleeping beside her, nestled on Eva's coat and tucked into the curve of her body. She put her hand over the baby, fear chasing away the last traces of sleep. "Are Burian's men coming? Did they find us?"

He squeezed her shoulder. "Relax. We're fine. We're leaving so we can get to the rendezvous." He held out his hand. "Let me help you up so you don't strain your wound."

She clasped his fingers and levered herself up, trying not to disturb Katya. "Is the storm over?"

"More or less."

"Where are Katya's things?"

"I stuffed them in my pack while you were sleeping," he said, nodding toward the door. The canvas knapsack that he'd taken his medical supplies out of leaned beside the door frame. It was stretched so full it looked round. "They'll be easier to carry that way."

She was about to thank him when she realized there could have been another reason he'd taken care of the bundles. Had he wanted to search her belongings for the disk more thoroughly? Eva swung her legs over the side of the bed frame, shoved her hair out of her eyes and looked around for Katya's carrier. She spotted it on the floor beside the fireplace. "Would you pass me the carrier, Sergeant Norton? I'd like to disturb Katya as little as possible."

Instead of releasing her hand, he tugged her to her feet. "Sorry, I can't let you use it. Your wound—"

"My wound is fine. The bleeding stopped hours ago." She looked back at Katya, then inhaled sharply as she was struck by a wave of dizziness. She tightened her grip on his hand. "How far do we need to go?"

"Around another twenty klicks," he replied.

"Will the people in the helicopter be there? I thought we'd missed the time."

"They'll be there tonight. The timetable just got pushed back twenty-four hours. We arranged a backup extraction scenario when we planned the mission. We try to cover every contingency." He glanced at Katya. "Well, almost every contingency."

Eva tugged her hand free from his grip and went to pick up the carrier. She faltered when she saw the rusty-brown patch of dried blood on the cotton. She couldn't see the blood on her sweater because of the dark wool, and she avoided looking at the stained area on her blouse. But the sight of the carrier reminded her once again of how close the bullet had come to Katya.

"Dr. Petrova…"

"I won't risk keeping my baby unrestrained again." She grabbed the carrier, straightening one set of ties as she returned to the bed frame. "Traveling with her on my lap yesterday was foolhardy."

"So would putting this contraption back on," he said, snatching the carrier from her. "Those straps would rub directly on your wound."

"I'm not going to hold her in my arms for twenty kilometers, especially over roads like these. All it would take would be one bad bump or sudden stop and Katya would be hurled…." She paused until she regained control over her voice. "I've already exposed her to far too much danger," she said, holding out her hand. "This is the best way to protect her."

"We leave in six, Jack," Colbert said. He picked up his own rucksack and went outside. Ice-laden wind swirled in from the darkness, along with the rumble of an engine before the door slammed shut.

Sergeant Norton tossed Katya's carrier on the bed frame and unzipped his coat. "Those straps look long enough to go around me. Show me how to fit the kid inside."

"What?"

"I'll carry her."

"No, she's not familiar with you. When she wakes up—"

"You'll be right beside her." He dropped his coat on the floor. "I agree that having her restrained is the best way to keep her safe. Since you can't do it, I will."

"But—"

"The longer you argue about it, the more danger we're all in."

What he said was true. Her objections were because of her own needs, not Katya's. She hadn't been more than a few steps away from her daughter since the baby's birth. It had always been just the two of them.

"Sooner or later, you're going to need to trust me, Dr. Petrova."

Did she? No, she knew better than that. Eva slid her hands beneath Katya to ease her into her snowsuit. Then she put on her hat and mittens and moved her as gently as possible to the pouch in the center of the carrier. "Trust has nothing to do with it, Sergeant Norton," she said. "This is a matter of expedience."

"Call it what you like as long as we get moving."

She eyed his height. "I'll be able to manage this better if you sit on the bed frame."

He complied and held his arms out at his sides. "Now what?"

"Hold her while I fasten the ties."

He brought his hands in front of him palms-up. "Okay, lay her on me."

The baby stirred when she was transferred to the sergeant's grasp. He held her stiffly until Eva put her hands over his and guided them toward his chest. "You need to keep her close. She likes feeling secure."

He spread his fingers over Katya's back and brought her against the front of his sweater. She snuffled, cuddled closer and settled back to sleep without opening her eyes.

Eva was surprised. Katya had calmed quickly the last time Sergeant Norton had held her, too. It hadn't been that way with Burian. The few times he'd picked her up, his daughter had begun fussing immediately. Eva leaned down so she could bring her face to Katya's. "What a good girl you are, kitten," she whispered. "I'll be right beside you. We're just going for another ride."

"You don't need to, uh, feed her again, do you?"

Eva could feel her cheeks heat at the mention of what had happened earlier. It had been a natural function, she reminded herself. It hadn't been sexual. So she shouldn't think about how close she was to his body. The fact that she was still holding her fingers over his didn't help. She grabbed the top set of straps and tied them behind his neck. "Not for a while."

"Because when you do, just let me know. I'll find you some privacy from the guys."

She blew her hair aside so she could focus on the knot she was making. "Thank you."

"No problem."

She put one knee on the bed frame. Taking care not to brush against him, she leaned behind him to bring the remaining set of straps behind his back. They barely met, so it took longer to tie them together. Finally, though, she managed to secure the carrier to her satisfaction. "There. That should hold," she said, pushing herself back to her feet.

He stood carefully, still cradling Katya with his hands. The ribbons from one of her mittens trailed over the back of his knuckles. He was obviously ill at ease holding the baby—like the other men, he'd be more accustomed to carrying weapons than children. Yet instead of looking awkward, he looked…endearing.

Eva scooped up his coat and held it out. "It's all right. You can let go of her now."

He took his hands away slowly, watching as the cotton carrier tightened with Katya's weight. "Man, she's tiny. Hard to believe she can make as much noise as she does."

"My daughter is the perfect weight for her size and her age." She thrust his coat at him and then retrieved her own and put it on. "And I think we already had the conversation about her healthy lungs."

"Easy there, ma'am. I wasn't insulting your kid." He zipped the front of his coat over Katya. "I just don't know anything about them."

Neither had she, until she'd had a baby of her own. She'd never envisioned herself as a mother, either. Her ambitions had involved having her own research project, not her own family. She placed her hand over his to stop him from closing his coat all the way so she could tie the loose ribbon on Katya's mitten. She pressed a quick kiss to the top of her head, then straightened up and looked around. "Have you seen my hat?"

He splayed his hand over the bulge Katya made as he stooped to reach beneath the bed frame. "Here."

She twisted her hair to cram it under her hat. "Let me know if you feel her begin to wake up. She'll often calm down when she hears my voice."

"Sure." He brushed a strand of stray hair off Eva's cheek with his fingertips. For a moment his thumb lingered at the corner of her mouth before he tucked her hair under the edge of her hat.

The caress caught her off guard. He was focusing on her lips.

And just like that, her body tingled with feelings that weren't remotely maternal. He was looking at her as if he wanted to kiss her. As if he cared. As if there weren't a truck full of armed men waiting outside.

No. He was a soldier, doing his duty. She was merely part of the mission to him, regardless of how good his touch felt. Or how much she wanted to lean into it. She tipped her head away. "We're ready to go, Sergeant Norton."

"Right." He dropped his hand. Without another word, he extinguished the lamp, picked up his pack and led her outside.

By the time dawn broke, the wind had died, leaving the air sharp but no longer biting. Daylight revealed slopes that bore a rugged mix of gray-black, windswept rock and crumbled stones. Apart from sharp-edged drifts where the road wound through treed valleys, most of the snow from the previous night's storm had blown clear. Puddles were already beginning to form in the ruts. So far, the team hadn't encountered any traffic, but that wouldn't last much longer. Ideally, they would have traveled in the dark so there would have been less chance of encountering other vehicles or having someone witness—and remember—the direction they took. Moving by daylight was always risky, yet that sheep farm had been too close to the complex so remaining there until nightfall would have been riskier.

Jack braced his boots against the floor to steady himself as the truck rocked around another curve. The engine sputtered. Maybe to a trained ear it would sound better after Kurt's tinkering, but it still seemed to Jack as if it would rattle apart at any minute. Considering the condition of the road and the vehicle, it wouldn't be wise to push for more speed.

But going slow was the last thing Jack wanted. The kid was no longer the limp weight she'd been when he'd strapped her on. He could feel her starting to stir against his chest. He sure hoped that didn't mean she was about to launch into one of her crying fests.

He leaned forward and twisted his head so he could see Eva's face. She was propped against his shoulder, her eyes still closed. Though she'd tried to fight it, she'd gone back to sleep shortly after they had started out. It was just as well that she'd let him carry the baby. The night had obviously taken its toll on her. Rather than wake her up to tend to her daughter, he opened his coat enough so that he could slip his hand inside the way he'd seen her do and placed his fingers over the curve of the baby's back.

The kid went still. Encouraged, Jack gave her a few pats for good measure.

"Too bad Gonzo's up front."

Jack looked up to find Tyler watching him. "What?"

"I think he'd consider the fifty bucks you cheated him out of worth it if he could see this."

"What are you talking about? I won fair and square. We were ready before Kurt was."

"That's because you're carrying the kid yourself."

"That wasn't cheating."

"What would you call it?"

"Expedience," Jack said, using Eva's word.

"Hey, Duncan," Tyler said. "Doesn't Jack look cozy there?"

Duncan nodded. "Uh-huh. Like a regular Father Goose."

Jack snatched his hand away from Katya. As soon as he did, though, she started to whimper. He patted her back again, and she quieted. "Come on, guys. I'm just doing what I have to. You've heard how loud this kid can get."

"He must have played with dolls when he was a boy," Tyler said, returning his attention to the road behind them. "What do you think?"

Duncan nodded. "Dolls are a well-known conditioning tool, used by females for centuries to indoctrinate the next generation of mothers."

"You guys in Intelligence have way too much time on your hands if that's the kind of information you come up with," Jack muttered.

"That's how my sister got started with her basic parent training," Duncan continued. "She had this baby doll she hauled around everywhere with her."

"I heard Jack didn't really want to be a medic, Dunk. His first choice was being a nurse."

"That explains it. Hey, Jack. Was it a nurse doll you played with?"

Jack heaved a sigh as the guys got going. He wouldn't hear the end of it now. He needed a diversion. "Junior's still playing with dolls, except they're the blow-up kind. They're the only dates he can get."

Duncan raised one eyebrow. "He does have a way with things that blow up."

"Something's glinting. Off to the northeast."

At Tyler's warning, Duncan sobered quickly. "Air or ground?"

"Air. The sun's behind it, so I can't make it out yet."

"The chopper should be coming in from the west. That's not one of ours."

Duncan tapped a few keys on his computer. "Base hasn't picked up any alarms from the complex. No chatter about a missing scientist or talk about pursuit."

Jack firmed his grip on the baby. "Tell Lang to floor it."

"We don't want to attract unnecessary attention if it's just a routine flight."

"That Ryazan guy is supposed to be a genius. All those scientists are, including Eva."

"That's right."

"So when he does find out that she's gone, he'll know she had help."

"He's right, Duncan," Tyler said. "Because of that patrol we ran into, Ryazan will know what we're driving, too."

"And since he's a genius," Jack continued, "what do you want to bet that he's smart enough to figure out we're monitoring their communications?"

It didn't take them long to grasp the situation. "Aw, hell," Duncan muttered. "They could have been maintaining radio silence like us." He stretched his arm and rapped on the window to the cab, signaling Kurt to go faster.

Jack slid his free arm around Eva and anchored her to his side as the truck picked up speed.

Either the increased jouncing of the truck or the shift in position woke her. She lifted her head and twisted to look at him. Though her eyelids were heavy and puffy, her eyes sparked with anxiety, just like the last time she'd awakened.

"It's okay, ma'am," Jack said. "We're almost there."

She brought her hand to her chest. Panic flared on her face. "Katya!"

"She's fine. I've got her, remember?"

She blinked and then thrust her hand into his coat. Her fingers brushed his as she groped for the baby. "She's all right?"

"Fine," he repeated. "I think she's waking up."

"Yes, she would be getting hungry soon."

He put his hand over hers. "Sorry, ma'am. This wouldn't be the best time…"

"I can see it now," Tyler said. "It's a chopper all right, but it's too small to be ours."

Over the noise of the truck, Jack heard the throb of the helicopter's engine. It wouldn't need to follow the twists of the road, so there was little hope of outrunning it.

"What's happening?" Eva asked.

"You might want to hang on to the strap again, ma'am." He squeezed her fingers and withdrew their hands from his coat. It was a good thing she had insisted on having the baby restrained in the carrier. Neither of them would be able to hold on to her adequately. "I have a feeling things are going to get bumpy."

"They're coming up fast," Tyler warned.

Eva fell against Jack's shoulder as the truck took a bend on two wheels. The helicopter was close enough for Jack to see it through the gap in the canvas. It was skimming the ridge above the road, sun glinting from its bulbous windshield and royal blue fuselage.

"Doesn't look like army issue to me," Duncan said. "Not unless the Russians are into painting their aircraft pretty colors."

"Oh, no," Eva cried. "It must be Burian's men. The complex's helicopter is that color of blue."

"Are you sure, ma'am?" Tyler asked.

"Yes! So are all their vehicles. Burian likes to be noticed. It feeds his ego."

Tyler sat back so he could prop his elbow on his bent knee and took aim. Firing on Russian troops, on Russian soil, would raise the profile of the mission past any chance of deniability. It could trigger an international crisis. Defending themselves against Burian Ryazan's private army was another matter entirely.

Light flashed from a point midway between the chopper's landing skids. The road behind erupted in plumes of slush and muddy dirt. Tyler returned fire, but the helicopter lifted out of range. The baby startled and began to wail.

"Eva, get behind me and stay down!" Jack ordered.

Instead of obeying him, she threw herself across his chest.

She was shielding the child, he realized. Damn, she was some woman. He wrapped his arm around her back and rolled over to reverse their positions. Once again, he ended up on his hands and knees on top of her. "Looks like we can forget about stealth, Duncan," he shouted over Katya's cries. He twisted his head to keep an eye on their pursuers. "You want to ask for a little help here?"

"I'm already on it, Jack." Duncan activated his transmitter and reported their situation in a few terse sentences.

"He's coming in for another run," Tyler warned, readying a pair of grenades.

An explosion rocked the truck. Eva screamed and clutched Jack's arms as slush and rock chips pelted the canvas. Tyler's second grenade exploded before it hit the road, putting out a shock wave that popped Jack's ears. "Dammit, junior, we've got a baby here," he yelled. "That's too risky."

"You got a better idea, Jack?"

The helicopter veered aside, then roared overhead. Jack gathered Eva closer, feeling the baby kicking between them, and braced himself. The canvas roof of the truck wouldn't slow bullets the way the metal sides would. Depending on the ammunition the complex equipped their guards with, his body might not be enough protection for Eva and her child, but it was the best he could do.

Yet the pain he'd anticipated didn't come. The helicopter went past the truck's unprotected roof and fired at the road in front of them.

"We're on our own, guys," Duncan said, pulling off his headphones. "They're sticking to the timetable. No evac until tonight."

Jack lifted his head to stare at him. "Say again?"

"You know the drill, Jack. They've got no choice. We're in too deep to risk a daylight flight. If they were identified they would compromise the operation."

Jack swallowed the rest of what he wanted to say. Duncan was right. Every man on the team accepted the risks when they went out. More often than not, Eagle Squadron did end up on their own. He swore and looked at Tyler. "Hey, junior. What's the chances of you bringing down that chopper without frying us in the meantime?"

"I could bring them down with a rock if they got close enough, but they're keeping their distance. It looks as if they're not even trying to hit us."

"They're not," Jack said. "They're only trying to stop us."

"Why?"

Jack looked from one man to the other. "They know we have Eva and Ryazan's baby in this truck," he said. "He wants them back alive."

Eva dug her fingers into his arms. "It's Katya he wants, not me."

Jack focused on Eva. Her hat had come off. Her hair fanned around her head in a halo of platinum. It was an irrelevant detail. He didn't know why he noticed it. Other than it looked all wrong against the bark and rust flecks of the truck bed. It was as pale as her baby's. It was as soft as a whisper where it flowed over his wrists.

Her expression wasn't soft, though. It was as fierce as a warrior's. She lifted her head from the floor to bring her face closer to his and spoke through her clenched teeth. "You can't let him take her. Whatever happens to me, promise you won't let Burian take my baby."

Jack didn't like to make promises. In fact, he'd been careful never to promise a woman anything. Yet there was no way in hell he was going to let Burian Ryazan get his hands on either Eva or her child.

But that's because protecting her was his mission. His duty. That was all.

He nodded once, then he peeled her fingers off his

arms and sat back on his heels. "I have an idea. The way I see it—" His words were drowned out by a renewed burst of crying from Katya. He put his palm over her back and jiggled her a few times before he could speak again. "Ryazan's men are going to keep following this truck until we stop or run out of gas, right guys?"

"Or until they get ground reinforcements," Duncan said.

"Okay. Let them."

Eva grabbed his shoulder. "What do you mean? Surely you don't plan to abandon us."

He clasped her hand and tugged her toward the tailgate. "It's the other way around, Eva. We're going to be the ones doing the leaving."

Chapter 5

Eva crouched behind a boulder and fought to catch her breath. She could see nothing through the cloud of smoke and dirt that hung over the road, but she could hear the growl of the truck's engine as it accelerated away from her and the whining throb of the helicopter. There were three more explosions in quick succession. She slapped her hands over her ears, pressing closer to the boulder while more debris blew past.

Sergeant Norton had told her the grenades that Matheson was throwing would provide both a diversion and a smoke screen. So far, it was working as the men had planned. No one appeared to have noticed her leap from the truck. Cautiously, she uncovered her ears. It sounded as if the helicopter was farther away. She knew she shouldn't move until there was no risk of Burian's men seeing her.

But dear God, she couldn't hear Katya.

The sergeant should have been right behind her. Had she misjudged him? It had been his idea to use the truck as a decoy. He'd sounded so sure this would work. The other men had approved of the strategy, too, even though it had seemed remarkably simple. Without her and Katya to worry about, they were confident they would be able to neutralize the helicopter, as they put it. In the meantime, while Burian's men chased the truck in one direction, Sergeant Norton would escape with Eva and her daughter in the other.

What if he hadn't jumped in time? What if he'd injured himself when he'd landed? What if he'd fallen on Katya?

No! Oh, God! No! She couldn't bear the thought of either of them hurt. She loved her child more than her life. And the sergeant... She swallowed against a lump in her throat. No, she wouldn't want any harm to come to him, either. It wasn't just because he was now her only hope for reaching safety.

Eva could still hear the helicopter, but she didn't care. She shoved herself away from the boulder and peered at the road. "Sergeant Norton?"

The breeze was beginning to blow the smoke away, revealing scorch marks and gouges between the ruts on the road surface. The truck was already out of sight around a bend. The road was empty except for an oblong, mud-streaked object that lay on a thin layer of snow beside a puddle....

She wasn't conscious of racing forward. She couldn't even think until she reached the puddle and saw that the object was only the sergeant's pack. She picked it up and looked around. "Sergeant Norton?" she called.

The helicopter glinted in the distance, a flash of royal blue against the streaks of gold in the dawn sky. It banked to the right and vanished behind a ridge of black rock. The beat of its propeller faded, only to be replaced by the sound of running footsteps.

The sergeant was jogging down the road toward her, the sides of his coat flying open. He didn't appear to have been hurt. He moved with ease in spite of the fact he held his rifle with one hand and was cradling Katya to his chest with the other. The baby was still in her carrier. And she wasn't making a sound.

Eva dropped the pack and sprinted to meet them. She slid to a stop and grabbed his arms. "What happened? What's wrong with…" Her words trailed off when Katya turned her head, pulled her thumb from her mouth and smiled.

Air rushed back into Eva's lungs so quickly that she felt faint. She dropped her forehead against the sergeant's shoulder. A sound pushed at her throat, trying to get out, but she couldn't tell whether it was a sob or a laugh.

He let go of Katya and ran his palm over Eva's back. "Are you okay?"

She nodded against his coat.

"Did the jump do any damage?" he asked, opening her coat. Before she realized what he intended, he slipped his hand under her sweater and touched his fingertips to her side over the bandage. "It still feels dry. That's good. Does it hurt? You seem wobbly."

She shook her head. He'd instructed her to protect her side with her arm and roll when she landed. She had no memory of what she'd done. "Don't worry about me. How's Katya?"

He withdrew his hand and stroked Eva's hair. "The squirt's fine. Her mittens came off. That's all. I've got them in my pocket. You told me that she wouldn't break, remember?"

Yes, that's what she'd told him. It had seemed like so long ago since she'd said that, but less than a day had passed. She'd been so determined to act strong. What had happened to her resolve to show no weakness?

"I think she enjoyed it when I ran. She made a noise that sounded like a giggle. On the other hand, it could have been gas."

She blinked at a rush of tears. "When I couldn't find you and I couldn't hear her, I thought…"

"I know." He wrapped his arm around her, pulling her against his side. "I'm sorry I worried you. I jumped later. I wanted to wait for a snowdrift to cushion my landing so she didn't get hurt."

She watched as Katya found her thumb again and started sucking in earnest. "Thank you."

"I'm pretty sure she liked the jumping part, too. Maybe we should do it again. If she gets cranky I can climb on a rock or something and—"

Eva thumped his shoulder with her fist and raised her head. "This isn't funny."

He smiled. "Your daughter's a real trouper, Eva." He wiped his knuckle across her cheek. "She's almost as brave as her mother."

"I'm not brave."

He kissed her forehead. "You are downright awesome."

She didn't know what surprised her more, the compliment or the kiss. "Sergeant Norton…"

"Call me Jack," he said.

No. She shouldn't think of him as Jack. He had to remain the sergeant, no matter how beautiful his smile was. It crinkled the corners of his eyes and deepened the lines around his mouth. It made his gaze sparkle, and it made her heart want to smile back. How was she supposed to remember he was only doing his duty and that his consideration wasn't personal? How could she keep from liking him?

Then again, clinging to the formality hadn't stopped her from developing feelings for him anyway, had it? How many times had he shielded her now? He'd held her, he'd let her sleep on his shoulder. He understood her worry about Katya and tried to comfort her. He even tried to make her laugh. "Sergeant—"

"Jack," he repeated more firmly, pressing his forefinger to her lips. His smile faded. "The first thing we need to do is find some transportation. To do that, we'll need to head for the nearest town. If you slip and someone hears you address me by my rank, it's going to attract negative attention."

She fought the desire to part her lips over his finger. It felt natural to touch him, to lean on him, to share his warmth and his strength...

His words finally registered. He wasn't inviting her to use his first name out of friendship. It was so he could achieve his mission. What on earth was she thinking?

Her feelings for him couldn't be real, she reminded herself. They were a product of the circumstances and adrenaline. That's why her heart was beating so fast. And there was their almost constant proximity. She was losing track of the number of times she'd felt his body against hers. This was only a physical reaction. She could control it. She *had* to control it.

Eva jerked away from his touch and went to retrieve the pack.

The café was at the edge of a square paved with pockmarked stones in a town whose name Jack didn't even try to pronounce. Judging by the crowd of customers inside and the number of vendors who had set up stalls outside, it was a market day. Which was a stroke of luck. With people coming into town to buy, sell or swap their goods, the presence of two additional strangers would be less likely to be noted. Jack glanced at the table closest to theirs. Currently, it was occupied by a pair of elderly men in dark woolen caps. They'd barely glanced at Jack and Eva as they'd sat down—their attention was solely on the plates of grilled sausages and boiled beets they were wolfing down.

Jack tore off a piece of bread to soak up the grease on his plate and looked across the table at Eva. She had insisted on holding the kid on her lap with one hand while she ate with the other. It didn't hamper her movements in the least—maybe mothers were accustomed to functioning one-handed. She was digging into her food with as much enthusiasm as the old men.

He was relieved to see that her appetite was healthy. It had been almost midday by the time they'd reached town, since Eva had needed to stop twice along the way to tend to the baby—first to feed her and then to change her diaper. Though she'd tried to match Jack's pace, he'd seen that her energy had been flagging and it had worried him.

"Feeling better?" he asked. He kept his voice low out of habit, but the chances of anyone overhearing them were next to nil. Because of the noise from the other customers and the folk music blaring from the transistor radio behind the counter, Jack hadn't been able to hear what the men at the next table were saying or even what language they were speaking.

Eva nodded as she swallowed another mouthful. "Much better, thanks. I needed this."

"How's your wound? Any pain? Does it feel hot?"

"No, it's fine."

"You need to tell me if it isn't, Eva. You can't afford to get sick."

"I understand." She stabbed a chunk of sausage and chewed it thoroughly. "I looked under the bandage after I nursed Katya. It's fine," she repeated.

"I'd like to examine it again myself when we're done here."

Her cheeks immediately pinkened. "Really, that's not necessary. There's nothing to see."

She was wrong about that. There was plenty to see— only it wasn't what he should be looking at.

It had taken all of Jack's self-control to give her the privacy she'd asked for while she'd breast-fed the baby. He'd thought it was for the best. They had a long way to go together, and now more than ever he couldn't afford to let his concentration lapse. He should be thinking of her as a mission objective instead of a woman. "I'm concerned that you seemed faint."

"That's because I was hungry." She gestured toward the baby. "It takes a lot of calories to produce milk."

All right. That could explain her decreased energy. It wasn't due to a medical issue, only a maternal one. Jack shoved another piece of bread in his mouth and tried not to picture Eva's breasts filling with milk.

The trouble was, everything else about her seemed just as sensual. If he wasn't obsessing over her breasts, it was her hair. She'd stuffed it back under her hat before they'd come into town as an attempt to make herself less memorable, but it was too fine to stay in place for long. One piece had slid over her ear and dangled beside her jaw to frame her face. It shifted each time she chewed, drawing his attention to her mouth. And if he wanted to maintain even a shred of professionalism, he definitely shouldn't be looking at her lips.

She was a beautiful woman. Not because of her individual features, although her eyes were a spectacular blue, her skin was flawless and her cheekbones would make models envious. No, Eva's appeal came from what was inside. Her determination was attractive and so was her courage. Even her devotion to her child added to her appeal.

How could he have thought of her as an ice princess? There was plenty of heat beneath the surface. She wasn't immune to this physical thing between them, either. Those blushes of hers proved it.

"Where do we go from here, Jack?"

He had plenty of ideas on that, starting with seeing the rest of her, preferably when she wasn't holding the baby. Considering all the passion she'd shown so far, Eva wouldn't be a passive lover....

Man, he had to try harder to keep his mind on business. He slid his plate aside and leaned across the table. "I've got maps and a GPS unit in my pack, along with a wad of rubles. Once we get transportation, we're going to head for the rendezvous. We'll wait for our evac there."

She appeared to consider that for a while. Some of the tension in her shoulders began to ease. "It sounds as if you came well prepared," she said.

"Uh-huh. Getting separated from the team is just another one of those contingencies we like to plan for. We're all expected to be able to reach the rendezvous on our own."

"I hope the rest of the men aren't in trouble. What if Burian's men decide to fire on them after all?"

"I'd put my money on our guys any day. They'll

probably meet up with us before our chopper gets in, but if they don't, they'll find some other way to get home."

"But—"

"Don't worry, Eva. We're professionals. We do this kind of thing all the time."

She stopped chewing and looked at him. "Why?"

"Why? Because that's what we're paid for."

"I don't think so. We've known each other less than a day, and already you've risked your life at least twice for mine. This isn't simply a job for you."

"Hey, some guys hang glide or climb mountains."

"Are you saying you *enjoy* the risk?"

"It can be a rush. It makes me feel alive."

She shuddered. "Not me. I go out of my way to avoid adventures. I like my routines."

"Could have fooled me. You and the pipsqueak are doing great at this."

"I would prefer being in a nice safe office with a stack of journals any day to getting shot at and jumping out of moving trucks."

"Do I know how to show a girl a good time or what?"

She was startled into a laugh. It was a liquid, sweet sound, and it pleased Jack far more than it should have. He enjoyed making her smile, mostly because he could see that she tried to resist it.

As she did now. She shook her head and stabbed her last piece of sausage with enough force to make the fork squeak across her plate. "We're completely different, Jack."

He wanted to argue with her about that, but he wasn't sure why. They *were* different. He couldn't think of one thing that they had in common. "What made you decide to become a scientist, anyway?"

"Probably the chemistry set my father gave me for my sixth birthday."

"Didn't you play with dolls? I thought all girls had dolls."

"That sounds very sexist."

"No way. I'm an enlightened kind of guy. It's just something I heard."

"Then it's not entirely accurate. From the time I went to live with my father, I wasn't allowed to play with dolls. I had plenty of books, though. He believed all toys should have an educational value. He encouraged me to expand my mind."

"You went to live with him when you were only four."

She lifted one shoulder. "He raised me how he thought best. As it turned out, I had an aptitude for numbers."

"Well, I guess that would help."

"I liked them because they behave predictably, as long as you know the correct formula. When I was growing up, numbers were..." She trailed off and shook her head. "It's not important."

"Tell me anyway. What about numbers?"

She finished her sausage and put down her fork. "They were like people to me."

"Okay, you're going to have to explain that one."

"My father moved frequently from one position to another. He was often away. There were always new nannies and new schools to get used to. New languages, too. But the numbers never changed. They behaved the same whatever country we were in. I always recognized them. Their properties were like personality traits, so they were familiar to me, like..."

"Friends," he finished for her.

She gave him a half smile. "That wasn't in my file, was it?"

"No. Our intel is good but not that good."

"What about you, Jack?"

"Me? I flunked math. The only time numbers get my attention is when they have to do with odds."

"Odds? Ah, you mean with bets." She popped another chunk of bread into her mouth.

He smiled as he watched her eat. He didn't think she realized she'd started into his bread. "One of my great-great something grandfathers fought for the Confederacy in the Civil War. After the war ended, he became a professional gambler and worked the riverboats up and down the Mississippi. Taking risks is in my blood."

"Perhaps being a soldier is in your blood, too."

"It is. I drifted around for years until I found a home with the army."

"What about the rest of your family? Are they in the military, too?"

"Absolutely. You've already met my brothers."

"You regard your teammates as your family?"

"It's where I belong."

She tilted her head to study him. "Then perhaps we're not so different after all."

"How's that?"

"We both made our work our lives. We feel that's where we belong."

"Huh. I guess you're right about that."

"I loved my work at the complex. I went to live there shortly after my father died, and I regarded many of my colleagues as my family." She clenched her hand on the table. "But then I learned what a fool I'd been."

He reached out to cover her hand with his. "Stop beating yourself up about your research, Eva. You're not the only one Ryazan fooled. How do you think the Nobel committee are going to feel when they find out what he's been working on lately?"

"He was able to deceive so many people because he believed his own press. He's convinced he's a humanitarian."

"Even though he's developing a weapon of mass destruction?"

"Especially because of that. His parents survived the siege of Stalingrad during the Second World War but carried terrible emotional scars from what they endured. Burian was raised on stories of the horrors and deprivations of war. He believes the Chameleon Virus will cause less suffering than conventional weapons because it kills quickly and leaves no maimed or wounded."

"That's some twisted thinking."

"Not to him. He considers it perfectly logical. People can be slaughtered with precision. The virus doesn't require an army, either. A handful of individuals can eliminate the targeted population while leaving the buildings and infrastructure undamaged. And because the virus is completely stable when not in a host, there's no danger of accidental contamination while distributing it and no hot zone to contend with afterward." Her voice faltered. "Burian considers it...merciful."

Jack pursed his lips in a silent whistle. He understood now why this mission had been given top priority. "It sounds like a terrorist's dream weapon."

"It's a nightmare."

"How did you find out the truth, anyway?"

"Burian told me himself a month ago."

"Why?"

"He'd wanted to renew our personal relationship and

had thought I would be impressed with his cleverness. He'd assumed as a scientist I would appreciate the logic behind what he'd done. He was trying to appeal to my intellect."

"His version of flowers and candy."

"I suppose so."

"He took a big risk telling you."

"I'm not sure that he realized it. He's so convinced he's right that he can't conceive of anyone disagreeing with him. I pretended to go along with the research while I searched for a way to stop it." She looked at Katya. "My, God. I was such a fool."

"We all make mistakes."

"My daughter was not a mistake."

"I never said that."

"She is the most precious gift—"

"Eva, stop." He squeezed her hand. "I meant getting mixed up with Burian Ryazan was the mistake, not your baby. I can see how much you love her. No one would ever doubt that."

She closed her eyes, then sighed. "I'm sorry, Jack. I shouldn't be so defensive. But until I learned I was pregnant, I'd never pictured myself with children. It wasn't part of my plan for my life."

"I find that hard to believe. You seem as if you were meant to be a mother."

She shook her head. "I believed that marriage and children weren't for me. I'd convinced myself that my work was all I needed. I was good at it, too. I used to put a hundred percent of my energy into my career. It was Katya who showed me what I'd been missing."

This was something else they had in common, Jack realized. He'd always known he wasn't the type to settle down.

He'd inherited more than his loyalty to the army and his luck with cards from his rebel ancestor. He'd also inherited the Norton men's wanderlust. His own father hadn't stuck around long enough to see Jack's first birthday, although he'd breeze back through town every few years when he was on a winning streak and was flush with cash. He'd come loaded with presents like jewelry and fancy clothes for his wife and top-of-the-line baseball gloves and bicycles for Jack. Life was one long party during the times Beau Norton had been around.

Not that he had taught Jack how to oil the leather baseball glove and wrap it around a ball to break it in, or even how to throw a ball. He hadn't taught him how to ride a bike, either. Jack had watched how the other kids in the neighborhood had done it and had managed to pick it up on his own. There sure hadn't been any educational toys, unless he counted the decks of cards that he'd find around the house. Whenever the old man had been home, Jack's mother had been so focused on her husband that no one had cared whether or not Jack went to school. The only thing Beau had taught his son was how to look out for himself.

No, he'd taught him something else, too. Certain men weren't cut out to be husbands and fathers, and the earlier they realized that, the better it was for everyone.

Jack had grown up seeing how much damage a man's broken promises could do to a woman. His mother had lived for the times when her husband would return. For the few weeks or months he was there, she would wear his latest gifts with giddy pride, her love for him glowing from her face, painful and naked to see. And when he left, nothing would shake her faith that he would return, even when she had to pawn the jewelry to pay the rent and later couldn't find the will to get out of bed or to feed herself.

It had been tough for a kid to witness. Jack had wanted to help her, to save her, but he hadn't known how. Each time the cycle had repeated, a little more of her died. Although it was cancer that had taken her in the end, she'd given up long before she'd been diagnosed. It was a good thing Beau Norton hadn't come back for his wife's funeral. If Jack had seen him then, he probably would have killed him.

"Jack?"

He realized he was still holding Eva's hand. She'd turned it over so that she was clasping his. Katya was nestled against her other arm, her tiny hands wrapped around Eva's fingers. For an instant he imagined he could feel the baby's grip, too, as if he was connected to both of them.

"Is something wrong?"

Damn right, there was. For starters, now that Eva had finished eating, he should get them out of here instead of sitting around, enjoying her company, as if they really were a couple in town for market day as they were pretending to be. Regardless of the charade, he had no business touching her so much. He might have known her for less than a day, but it was crystal clear she wasn't his type of woman. She wouldn't be satisfied with merely sex and a good time. She and her baby were a package deal. If she ever decided to take a chance on another man, she'd be in it for the long haul.

And Jack wasn't. The final lesson he'd learned from Beau Norton was that the apple didn't fall far from the tree. He was just like his father, only he wasn't going to repeat his father's mistakes. He knew that the Norton men were too restless to make good husband or father material, so marriage and children weren't in the cards for him. Eagle Squadron was his family, and his work was all he needed.

Unlike Eva, he wasn't about to change his mind.

Chapter 6

The watchtower stood at the crest of the hill, the setting sun mellowing its weathered stone walls to burnished gold. Narrow windows were set high beneath the eaves where centuries ago sentries would have kept watch over the road that wound through the valley. The remains of what had once been buildings clung to the slope below the structure near a grove of pine trees. Here and there an intact wall thrust through the grassed-over mounds of rubble, but from where Eva stood, she could see little that was identifiable.

The site was one of the many medieval outposts that had dotted the Greater Caucasus. Some of the better preserved ones were still inhabited, either by descendants of the original villagers or by squatters, but not this one. The only movements visible were tree branches that the wind caused to scrape against the ruined walls and birds that flitted through the gaping windows of the tower.

Eva held Katya to her shoulder, rubbing her palm over the baby's back. This was the rendezvous point the team had chosen. As Jack had explained, it would give them some shelter while they waited. It was also a good landing spot and was isolated enough from the surrounding towns to ensure privacy. Sometime before dawn, a helicopter should be setting down on the bare rock of the hilltop. Whether the rest of the Eagle Squadron team showed up in time to meet it or not, Eva would carry her daughter on board and begin the final leg of their journey.

It was almost over. Thank God.

"You need to get under cover, Eva."

She turned toward Jack's voice, then had to take a quick sideways step to maintain her balance. She must have moved too fast. She firmed her grip on Katya and watched Jack approach. He held his rifle in one hand and had his pack hooked over his shoulder, along with a red- and brown-striped blanket. The car he'd used to drive them here was nowhere in sight.

"I was waiting for you," she said. "Where did you find that blanket?"

"It was in the car trunk. I thought it would be useful."

She glanced past him. "What happened to the car?"

"I cut some pine boughs to put over it. No one should be able to spot it from the air or the ground."

"I wish there was somewhere we could leave it so the owner could get it back."

He cupped her elbow when he reached her. "Someone will find it eventually."

"But you had money. The people in that town appeared to have so little—"

"Eva, if I bought it, someone would remember us for

certain and be able to describe us to Ryazan's men. We don't know when they'll start looking in this direction, but it's a sure bet they will."

She knew he was right. Their survival was at stake, and she would do a lot worse than steal in order to protect Katya. Considering the horror she'd helped develop at the complex, it was absurd to have conscience pangs about stealing a car.

"We're not in the clear yet," Jack continued. He turned her toward the tower and urged her forward, guiding her to walk where the wind had swept the snow from the hillside. "I don't want to underestimate your boyfriend. If I were him, I'd be pretty determined to get you back."

"I told you. It's Katya he wants, not me."

"I wouldn't be so sure about that."

"There are other scientists on the project who can continue where I left off. And since I did leave, he would have to know that I would no longer cooperate. I'm of no further use to him."

"I wasn't talking about your professional relationship, Eva."

"I already told you, the personal relationship I had with Burian is over. It ended well before Katya was born."

"Maybe not in his opinion. He told you about the virus so he could win you back."

"Well, it didn't work. And I would appreciate it if you don't refer to him as my boyfriend."

"Then what was he?"

It was a simple question, but she wasn't sure of the answer. Burian had once been her mentor. She'd liked and respected him. He'd given her a stable home at the complex after her father had died, and for a time it had seemed as if he'd wanted to step into that role for her. The

thirty-year gap in their ages had seemed unbridgeable
when she'd been nineteen. She wasn't sure when it had
begun to change, when her hero-worship had turned into
infatuation.

All she was sure of was that Burian had taken
full advantage of her innocence. She'd trusted him
completely. She'd thought she loved him, yet how could
she have when she hadn't really known him?

"He was many things to me," she replied finally. "But
it was only our working relationship that he truly valued.
That and his daughter."

Jack was still holding her elbow. He slid his fingers
along her arm until he touched Katya's back. "What
would a guy like that want with a baby? He doesn't sound
like much of a family man."

"He has a large ego, and he feeds it by exerting control
over the work at the complex and over the people who
surround him. I suspect he seduced me in the first place
in order to control me personally as well as professionally.
He wants Katya because she's his. That's all. He views
her as an achievement, a possession, not a child."

"Sounds like you would have left him anyway even
if you hadn't learned about the virus."

"That's true. Katya is my priority now, and I know
Burian would never have made a good father. She's better
off having no father than having one like him."

Jack looked from the baby to her, his expression
unreadable. Then he dropped his hand and increased
his pace. "Some guys are like that. Lucky for both you
and the kid that you figured it out when you did."

She suspected that what she'd said had bothered him.
She hurried to follow. "Jack?"

He stopped at the base of the tower. "Uh-huh?"

"I didn't lie to the government. I do want to expose Burian's research."

"Sure. I got that."

"I don't want you to think I've put you and your team in danger just because I wanted to leave my..." She stumbled over the word. "Leave Katya's father."

"Hey, I'm just following orders, remember? It wouldn't make any difference to me if you're running away because you were smuggling out his prize-winning cherry pie recipe." He pointed to the shadowed side of the tower. "Wait there. I won't be long."

"Where are you going now?"

"I need to check out the interior." He ducked his head to step through the low doorway. There was a sudden flurry of squawks and flutters before a handful of sparrows zoomed out. They were followed by something small and gray that scurried over the threshold. A few minutes later, Jack reappeared minus his pack and the blanket. He loped down the hill to the pine grove, and then he returned with a stack of boughs and motioned her to follow him inside.

The interior of the building was one large chamber with a floor of stone instead of packed earth as she'd expected. Dark holes along the walls were all that was left of the timbers that must have once supported a staircase. The roof was gone. Sunlight tinted the top round of stones and streamed through the window slits, illuminating the dust that floated through the air. Enough light filtered downward to reveal traces of turquoise and faded pink on the wall opposite the doorway.

Eva moved farther inside, her boots crunching through a drift of dead leaves. The colors were what was left of a painting. The tower was surprisingly intact, considering its age.

"It could get cold once the sun goes down," Jack said. He laid the pine boughs in a corner out of the draft from the door. "If it does, we might need to go back to the car and run the engine for a while."

"It doesn't seem too cold now."

"Not yet." He spread the blanket he'd brought earlier over the branches. "In the meantime, this should keep you comfortable when you have to feed the baby again."

She gritted her teeth as she felt the heat of yet another blush in her cheeks. It wasn't that he had embarrassed her. Over the course of the day, he'd become matter-of-fact about the necessities of Katya's care, something she was grateful for. He'd seemed almost as concerned with her welfare as Eva was.

But that hadn't stopped the effect he had on Eva's pulse whenever the topic of breast-feeding came up. "She seems content right now. I think all the activity has tired her out."

"If you're hungry, I've got some MREs in my pack. Just let me know."

"What's an MRE?"

"Sorry, army jargon. It's what passes for food in the field. I've got a full canteen, too."

"Thank you, but—" She stopped herself before she could refuse his offer. Now that she thought of it, her throat felt odd. Not dry but tight. She hoped there hadn't been something wrong with the sausages she'd eaten earlier. "If you wouldn't mind, I'd like some water."

He brought her the canteen, unscrewed the cap and held it out. "Want me to hold the pipsqueak?"

"No, thanks," she said, pressing Katya against her shoulder with one hand while she freed up the other. "I've had a lot of practice doing things one-handed."

"That's what I figured when I watched you eat."

"It's one of the skills of motherhood they didn't mention in the books I read." She put the canteen to her lips. As soon as she tipped back her head, the room spun. She staggered sideways.

Jack clasped her arms to steady her. "What's wrong?"

She blinked. "Nothing."

"Eva, you'd better lie down."

"No, I'm fine." She breathed deeply a few times, then managed to take a drink. "Thanks."

"You're wobbly again."

"I'm just tired."

"Maybe. Or maybe it's because of your wound. Damn. I knew I should have checked under the bandage. Come with me." He released her arms and plucked both the canteen and Katya from her grasp.

"Jack!" She made a grab for her baby, but he'd already moved out of reach. Rather than being upset by the sudden change of position, Katya gurgled and waved her arms.

Eva scowled, even though she knew she should be happy that her child didn't fuss when Jack held her. "I know you mean well, Jack, but—"

"The sooner we get started, the better." He knelt on the floor beside the makeshift pallet and set the baby down on the blanket. Then he yanked off his coat and tucked it around her. "We have less than an hour of daylight left."

Katya kicked the coat away and grabbed her feet, squealing in glee as she looked at Jack. He seemed disconcerted for a moment. Then he opened his pack and pulled out his med kit. "Babies like shiny things, right, Eva?" he said over his shoulder. "Do you think she'd like to play with my scissors?"

She bolted across the room and reached past Jack's shoulder to place her hand between him and Katya. "You can't possibly mean to give scissors to…" She stopped when she saw his face. "I should have known you weren't serious."

"It got you over here, didn't it?" He caught her wrist and tugged her down to sit on the blanket beside the baby. Branches crackled beneath her, releasing the scent of pine needles. "Take off your coat," he said. "I'm going to look at that wound."

"But we'll be evacuated in a matter of hours."

"Sure, if everything goes according to plan. Murphy hasn't been too kind to us lately."

"Murphy?"

"More jargon. Anything that can go wrong, will."

"You're making a fuss over nothing. I told you it's fine."

He rose to his knees and pushed her coat off her shoulders. Then he sat back on his heels and took her hands in his. "Don't argue with me about this, Eva. I've seen scratches turn septic in the field, and what you got was a lot more than a scratch."

"Jack—"

"Humor me, okay?" He squeezed her knuckles. "I'm worried about you."

She looked down at their hands. Her resistance to his examination had nothing to do with her injury. She didn't want him to touch her. At the same time, she wanted more than anything to feel his hands on her body. Simply the sensation of his fingers against hers was making her pulse speed. The thought of having him stroke the more delicate skin along her side…

What was wrong with her? He was a medic. This wasn't personal. She shifted so that her wounded side faced him and drew her sweater over her head. Her hair crackled and clung to her cheeks. She brushed it out of her eyes. Before she could reconsider, she undid the lower buttons of her blouse until she was able to draw the blood-stained fabric clear of the bandage. "Go ahead."

He cleansed his hands with an alcohol gel as he had before, leaned closer and gently peeled up the tape.

Cool air wafted across the wound, making her shudder. The numbing cream he'd put on the day before had worn off long ago. Though overall the area was nowhere near as painful as it had been when she'd first been injured, the exposed torn skin did sting. She focused on Katya and tried to ignore her discomfort. "Well?" she asked.

"It looks good so far, but it's hard to know for sure in this light."

She started to lower her blouse but he stopped her.

"Hang on," he murmured. He slid his fingertips along her rib cage above the wound and then did the same beneath it.

Eva bit her lip. Oh, his touch felt even better than it had the first time. The contact of his fingers seemed to take away the sting. The warmth that spread across her skin wasn't painful. It was stimulating.

He cleared his throat. "There doesn't seem to be any swelling. The area isn't hot."

"That means it's all right?"

Instead of replying, he leaned over to bring his face close to her side. He inhaled slowly.

She shuddered again, only it wasn't from the cold. Though he wasn't touching her now, she could sense his nearness more acutely than before. "What are you doing?"

"Smelling it. It's a low-tech way to check for infection."

"And?"

"All I can smell are pine needles." He leaned closer and inhaled more deeply.

How many times had she reminded herself that his actions weren't personal? It was hard to remember that when his face was less than an inch from her breast. She looked at his hair, imagining how it would curl around her fingers. Would it be soft? Or stubborn and wiry? His shoulders were so broad. She'd already felt how strong his arms were. One of his sleeves had pulled tight when he'd leaned over, and she could see the contour of his biceps beneath his sweater. Her palm tingled with the urge to stroke it….

She clenched her hands into fists. "Jack?"

He sat back on his heels. He didn't speak again until he had smoothed a fresh bandage into place. "You were right." His voice was rough. "There's no sign of infection. Looks like your symptoms are from plain old fatigue."

She buttoned her blouse and pulled on her sweater. "I hope you're satisfied."

He rubbed his face hard, and then he reached past her for her coat. Rather than handing it to her, he regarded the side where the bullet had passed through the wool fabric. "It's my duty to see to your needs, Eva," he said. "My own satisfaction, or lack of it, has no bearing on this mission."

"I understand that. It was just an expression."

He fitted his little finger into one of the holes in her coat. "You smell like honey."

"What?"

"The scent of your skin. It's sweet."

"Jack…"

"No, not exactly like honey. I'd have to taste it to know for sure."

The image sprang instantly to her mind. Jack's cheek resting on her stomach, her fingers tangled in his hair, her skin moist and tingling from his kisses. She'd already felt his lips on her forehead. That kiss had been too brief. What would it be like to feel his lips on her mouth? Or on her thighs?

"But you're under my protection, Eva, so my curiosity is only one of the things that won't get satisfied...." His voice trailed off. He poked his finger farther into the hole in her coat. "What's this?"

She was still immersed in the image of Jack tasting her. It took her a while to focus on what he was looking at. When she did, it brought her back to reality as effectively as a slap. She snatched her coat from him and got to her feet.

"Eva?"

She thrust her arms into her sleeves.

"There was something hard in there," he said.

"Maybe it was the bullet."

"Couldn't be. There were two holes. It would have passed through." He rose to stand in front of her. "It's the disk, isn't it?"

She stepped past him and bent over to reach for Katya.

He hooked his arm in front of her waist to pull her back up. "She's fine."

It was obvious that he was right. Eva knew the pine-bough pallet was soft, and it was warm enough to keep away the chill of the floor. Katya was still playing with her feet and in no distress. "Don't tell me how to handle my child."

"Then don't use her to change the subject." He turned her to face him and placed his hand directly over the place where she'd sewn the computer disk into the lining of her coat.

The gesture knocked her breathless. Not because he'd found the disk that she'd hoped to keep concealed but because his thumb was pressing the underside of her breast. If he moved his hand just a fraction of an inch, he would be cupping it.

"This isn't a good spot. It could have been damaged when you were hit."

Heaven help her. She wanted to lean into his touch. If she did, would it turn into a caress? She wanted to feel his hand on her naked skin again. She was sorry she'd put her coat back on....

What was wrong with her? She stepped back, breaking the contact. "Stop touching me. You're always touching me."

"I only touch you when it's necessary."

"As it was now? I should have realized this was a ruse."

"What are you talking about?"

She backed away. "You didn't really want to check my wound, did you? You wanted a chance to search my coat."

"That's ridiculous."

"You've been trying to get that disk from the time we met, haven't you? Those were your real orders, weren't they?"

"No, that's not true."

"You probably searched Katya's belongings before you put them in your pack."

"Eva—"

"Was that the real reason you insisted on carrying my baby? So you could make sure the disk wasn't in her carrier? Did you search her, too?"

He closed the distance she'd put between them and took her by the shoulders. "I already told you what my orders were."

"All this consideration you've been showing me, all this kindness, it was just to make me drop my guard."

"You're wrong, Eva."

"And like a fool I believed you cared. I should have known better. You're a soldier. You've told me yourself that all you care about is the mission."

"All I *should* care about is the mission."

"The information on this disk is my ticket to a new life. I'll hand it over to your government only when my daughter and I are safe."

"So you said yesterday. That's fine by me."

"Good. Let go of me, Sergeant Norton."

"Not until we get this straightened out. And my name's Jack."

"Not to me. You've found the disk. You don't have to pretend to be my friend anymore."

"I wasn't pretending anything."

"You can stop now. You got what you wanted."

He gave her a light shake. "Think, Eva. If I really had wanted to get that disk, I wouldn't have needed to play games. I would have searched you while you slept. Or I could have overpowered you and forced you to hand it over whenever I chose to. So why didn't I?"

Her throat felt too thick for her to formulate a reply. What he'd said was true. He was a head taller than her and likely outweighed her by at least sixty pounds. He was all lean muscle, moved like an athlete and was never unarmed. He indeed could have overpowered her with ease. At any time. Whether she'd been asleep or not.

The reminder should have frightened her. It didn't. Instead, it started to calm her.

"And tell me, Eva. Do you honestly believe it would have made a damn bit of difference if you'd handed over that disk when we met? Do you think I would have done anything differently? That I wouldn't have protected you? Or wouldn't have helped you?"

"I don't—"

He brought his face to hers before she could finish. "And regardless of my orders, do you really believe I'm enough of a bastard that I'd desert a woman and a helpless infant in the middle of hostile territory just because some pencil-pushing bureaucrat decided they were expendable?"

She had hurt him. She could see it in his eyes. That, more than his words, was what finally got through to her. She inhaled hard, straining for breath. Her senses filled with the scent of his body. Soap, wool and warm male skin. It was the same scent that had enveloped her each time he'd held her, each time he'd been willing to give his life to protect hers.

He didn't deserve her suspicions. He'd already proved himself to be an honorable man.

She shook her head. "Everything's happened so fast. Information was the only bargaining chip that I had. I've been afraid to trust anyone."

"I understand that you're scared." He eased his grip, rubbing his thumbs along the top of her shoulders. "You have every reason to be because you're running for your life. But I'm not your enemy."

She nodded. "I know, but—"

"And I'm sure as hell not Burian."

"Burian? This has nothing to do with him."

"Yes, it does. He's warped your view of all men. You trusted him, and he betrayed you. He turned the work you loved into a lie. He messed with your head so much that you assume the only thing he could want from you is your scientific expertise."

"I already told you that he would realize I would no longer cooperate."

"You're missing the point. You're a passionate, courageous, beautiful woman. A man doesn't need an ulterior motive to want to touch you."

"Jack…"

"And just for the record, I do care about you, Eva." He slid his hands to her face and cradled her cheeks in his palms. "But it would be a hell of a lot simpler if I didn't."

She could have moved away then. Or turned her face aside when he lowered his head. She did neither. She stood rooted to the floor and let him kiss her.

Oh, it shouldn't feel this good. They had just been arguing. She had been angry with him. She shouldn't trust him. She couldn't rely on her judgment when it came to men. She'd been so horribly wrong before.

The familiar refrain played through her head, but it had no effect. His kiss felt real. More than that, it felt natural. Right. Instead of being sensible and pushing him away, she found she had anchored her hands in the front of his sweater and was pulling him closer.

She should tell him it was only due to the circumstances, to their forced proximity, to excitement. The physical attraction was a consequence of chemistry. She still barely knew him. Yet before the thought finished forming, he slipped his tongue into her mouth and her brain simply shut down.

His taste was fresh like the springwater she'd drank from his canteen. It curled through her senses, seducing her as softly as the gentle pressure of his lips. She moaned at the pleasure and slid her hands to his shoulders.

At her response, he braced his feet apart, clasped her hips and pulled her flush to his body. Eva trembled, grateful for his firm hold. She'd felt his body against hers more times than she could count now, but this was different. This time, she allowed herself to enjoy it.

He was so firm, so solid, everywhere they touched. Her own body was responding instinctively. Blood was rushing to places that had rested dormant for months, stirring needs she'd tried to forget about when she'd entered motherhood. She wrapped her arms behind his neck to press her breasts to his chest. Her nipples hardened so swiftly she winced.

Something fluttered overhead. Probably a bird, trying to reclaim its home. Dirt gritted on the stone beneath her boots. Katya's whimper was fainter than either sound, but it was enough to enable Eva to regain her senses.

She broke off the kiss and gasped for air.

Jack moved his lips along her cheek to her ear. He licked the lobe, then rubbed it gently between his teeth.

"No," she breathed. "Stop."

"Eva…"

"This is a mistake, Jack."

He pressed his forehead against hers. "Yeah, I know."

His quick agreement surprised her. She had expected—wanted?—him to push her for more.

He sifted a handful of her hair through his fingers. "I should apologize. I took advantage."

"You didn't take anything." She dropped her arms to her sides. "I'm as much at fault."

"No. I've seen this happen before. Being in danger can scramble people's emotions. It's the adrenaline. We've had psych lectures about this, and I should know better."

He turned his face to her hair and inhaled. Then he released his hold on her and stepped back. "I was way out of line. It won't happen again."

She should be pleased. He was being sensible. He'd echoed what she'd already thought. There were so many reasons why she shouldn't kiss Jack that she couldn't begin to list them.

Yet she had to cross her arms over her chest so she didn't reach for him once more.

He went to where he'd left his gun, picked it up and walked to the doorway in silence. He didn't speak until he was on the threshold. "I'm going to tour the perimeter before the sun sets. You'll be safe here."

He was back in full soldier mode, she realized, his movements crisp, his voice firm. He was acting as if the kiss had never happened. She tried to follow his lead. "Take your coat," she said. "I'll use the blanket for Katya."

He laughed without humor. "No, thanks. I could use some cooling off."

"Jack?"

"This is my job, Eva. It's the only reason we're together. It's my duty to keep you safe, and I'm going to be damned sure that you are." He paused. "Especially from me."

Chapter 7

Jack leaned his back against the wall and propped his boot on the edge of the doorway, the familiar weight of his rifle in his hands. This was what he knew. It was what he was good at. It was the life he wanted. He was no different from countless other soldiers who had stood in this same spot over the centuries, their weapons at the ready, while they kept watch over the valley.

The designers of the outpost had chosen the site well. Though the moonlight illuminated the surrounding area, it didn't penetrate the shadows on this side of the tower. Even without being able to climb to the top and look out the windows, Jack still had the advantage over anyone who approached. So far, apart from the rustling of wildlife among the dried shrubs, and the occasional whisper from the pine grove when a breeze puffed through, the night had been dead quiet. No sign of pursuit. No trace of the evac helicopter yet, either. The only trouble was, the silence outside the tower made it that much harder to ignore the sounds that came from inside. For the past twenty minutes Eva had been nursing the kid.

Jack doubted whether any of the other soldiers who had stood here over the centuries had had a distraction quite like this one. Why was it that his senses were so finely attuned to everything that woman did? He thumped his head against the wall and told himself to ignore her.

It was no use. He could hear the pine branches shift as she changed position, and he tried not to imagine what she was doing on that blanket. Or to picture how the moonlight would filter through the top of the tower to gleam on her naked skin. He heard her murmur something to Katya, her voice taking on the special tenderness she used whenever she spoke to her child. And he tried not to remember the way she'd moaned deep in her throat when he'd given her his tongue.

Damn, he shouldn't have kissed her. Most of the time, he had no business touching her, either. Didn't seem to make any difference because he couldn't seem to stop.

With any luck, by tomorrow it would no longer be an issue. Eva and her cargo should be delivered to whatever government department awaited her. Their welfare would be out of his hands. She would go on to a new life in America. Jack would go on to the next mission. The information on the disk would be processed, the diplomats would do their thing and the world would be a safer place. Everyone would be happy.

A blur of movement to his left caught his eye. He turned and focused on the ruins that were partway down the slope. A rabbit crept from behind a crumbled wall, poked around nervously for a few minutes and disappeared beneath a bush.

Eva had been scared, too. Not timid like that rabbit, but just as conscious of the danger she'd been in. He'd realized that when they'd met. He'd seen proof of it again in her paranoid reaction when he'd found that disk.

But instead of making allowances for her less-than-rational state of mind, he'd kissed her.

He banged his head against the wall again. What had happened to his self-control? His honor? He'd known kissing her was wrong, but he'd enjoyed every second of it. To make matters worse, so had Eva. She sure didn't kiss like a scientist. There had been nothing cool or intellectual about her response. It was just as he'd suspected; she had plenty of passion. Too much passion for a man like Burian.

Jack thought of the photo he'd seen during the mission briefing. Burian Ryazan was white-haired, only a few inches taller than Eva and was lean to the point of gauntness. His features were honed sharp, his mouth a carved line, his eyes dark and calculating. He did look as if he would consider his child a possession. He'd likely regarded Eva that way, too. Jack couldn't picture the two of them together. Correction, he didn't want to picture them together. She deserved someone closer to her age, someone more physically compatible who could match her passion....

But it wasn't going to be Jack. No, sir. He knew what he wanted, and it wasn't a nesting woman with a ready-made family. Once this mission was over, he'd never see her again. Which was good. For both of them.

The rabbit bounded out from the concealment of the bush and streaked across the hillside. Jack froze, his senses going on full alert.

A new shadow had appeared halfway between the pine grove and the tower. Jack regarded it for a full minute, trying to determine if it was the result of the setting moon lengthening the shadow of one of the boulders. It remained motionless, but something about the shape wasn't right.

He crouched to make himself less of a target and brought his rifle to his shoulder. A thorough scan of the hillside revealed nothing else out of place. There was still no sound of an engine or anything mechanical. To be on the safe side, Jack took aim at a spot just behind the boulder.

An animal howled from the shadow Jack was targeting. Precisely five seconds later it howled again. And there was something familiar about it....

Jack blew out a relieved breath and eased his finger away from the trigger. "That's one lovesick coyote, junior," he called softly.

Tyler moved from behind the boulder and stepped into the moonlight. "It was a wolf."

"If you say so."

"Should have known a city boy like you wouldn't be able to tell the difference." He climbed the hill and stopped a few feet from the base of the tower. "Any problems?"

"No, the area's clear."

He turned to look behind him. "I saw the glint of your rifle. I wanted to make sure whose it was before I showed myself."

Jack took another look around, but he could see no one else. "Where are the others?"

"Lang is ditching the truck. Dunk and Gonzo are doing a sweep of the vicinity. They should be here in a few minutes."

"How'd you manage to lose the pretty blue chopper?"

"We found a spot just past a bridge on the side of a gorge and faked engine trouble. They came in close enough to shoot our roof off, so I was able to take out their tail rotor."

"That would have done it."

"Yeah. They spun right into the side of a cliff. Judging by the size of the fireball on impact, they didn't have that much fuel left."

"You said they targeted the roof?"

"It might have been accidental. There was some bad wind sheer over the gorge that made the chopper pitch. That old canvas shredded so fast. The wind did most of the damage."

"With the roof gone, they would have seen that Eva and the kid weren't on board."

"Maybe. Duncan couldn't tell whether or not they got a transmission off before they crashed. He was busy with damage control."

"What happened?"

"His computer took a couple of rounds right through the hard drive. Good thing he saved the radio."

"Damn, that's too close. It's lucky we bailed."

"Yeah. When Dunk saw what they'd done to his toy, he used some language no lady should hear." He paused. "Where is our lady, anyway?"

Jack tipped his head toward the doorway. "Inside."

"Can't stand your company already, huh?"

"She's breast-feeding the kid."

"Whoa."

Jack snorted. He'd said the same thing the first time. "Hey, Eva," he said, turning his head toward the doorway. "We've got company."

There was no reply.

Jack moved to the threshold and spoke again. "Eva? It's okay. They're the good guys."

Instead of Eva's voice, he heard a faint whimper from Katya. He slung the strap of his rifle on his shoulder and pulled his penlight from his pants pocket. "Stay here and keep watch, junior," he said, ducking his head as he stepped over the threshold.

He allowed his eyes a few moments to adjust, and then he moved toward the pallet in the corner. Katya continued to whimper, with still no sound from Eva. He switched on his light, directing the narrow beam toward the dark shape that lay on the blanket.

Eva was on her side, her eyes closed, her head pillowed on her bent arm while her other arm was curled around the baby.

Jack knelt beside her and pressed the underside of his wrist to her forehead to make sure she didn't have a fever. He hadn't found any hint of infection when he'd examined her wound, but that had been several hours ago. Thankfully, her skin felt cool. Her breathing was normal, too. By all appearances, this was a healthy sleep.

She stirred at his touch, her eyelids fluttering. "Jack?"

"Shh, it's okay," he said. He stroked a lock of hair off her cheek before he withdrew his hand. "I just wanted to tell you the guys are here."

"They made it? Are they all right?"

"Uh-huh. Go back to sleep."

"Katya…"

He placed his hand over Katya's stomach. The baby immediately quieted. "Don't worry. She's fine."

Eva's mouth moved into a smile that lasted only a moment before her lips parted on a delicate snore.

Jack played the light over her more closely. She must have fallen asleep as soon as she'd finished feeding the baby. She'd fastened her blouse, but her sweater was still pulled up. He set the flashlight on the blanket and carefully tugged down her sweater. He clenched his jaw, ordering himself not to linger, as his knuckles grazed the side of her breast. Moving quickly, he drew the sides of her coat closed and then pushed himself back to his feet.

As soon as he'd stood, Katya began fussing again.

"Something wrong, doc?" Tyler asked, ducking his head as he stepped through the doorway.

"Shh. Don't wake her up."

"Sounds like she's already awake."

"I mean Eva," Jack whispered. "She's exhausted."

"No wonder, having to put up with that kid. What a set of lungs on her."

Eva began to stir again. Before she could open her eyes, Jack leaned over to set down his gun and scooped the baby off the blanket. Katya switched from whimpering to gurgling. He waited until Eva's breathing had steadied once more. Then he moved toward Tyler. "All babies cry," he said, unconsciously repeating what Eva had told him the day before. "It's one of the ways they communicate."

Katya squirmed, drawing up her knees.

He hooked his hands beneath her armpits and held her away from him so he could look at her. Moments later, she emitted a loud belch.

Tyler snickered. "So, what's she saying now?"

Jack grimaced. Katya's belch had been accompanied by a mouthful of milk. It splatted down her stomach to drip on the toes of his boots. "Geez, do you think she's sick?"

"You're the medic. You tell me."

"For some reason, none of my field manuals included any chapters on barfing babies."

"At least she's quiet."

That was true, Jack thought. She actually seemed pleased with herself, so maybe she wasn't sick. "Why aren't you on watch?"

"Duncan and Gonzo are out there now. Lang was working his way up the hill when I came inside."

"Okay, then make yourself useful by holding the kid for a while," Jack said, thrusting the baby toward Tyler.

He backed up fast and held up his palms. "No way. She's your baggage."

"She likes to be held. It keeps her quiet."

Katya drew up her knees again. Jack angled her away so whatever came up with the belch wouldn't hit his boots this time, but it wasn't a burp that her efforts produced.

Tyler recoiled. "What's that smell?"

"Thought you'd be able to recognize it, junior, seeing as how you were raised on a ranch."

He fanned the air with his hand. "That's even worse than the noise. How can women want those things?"

Duncan moved through the doorway. "The chopper's on its way," he said. "ETA fifty minutes." He stopped. "Hey, Father Goose. Everything okay?"

"Keep your voice down," Jack said. He glanced back at Eva. Though he'd left the flashlight so that its beam wouldn't shine on her face, it gave enough light for him to see that her eyes were still closed. "Eva needs her sleep."

"She sure looks out of it. What's wrong with her?"

"Just exhaustion. Producing milk takes a lot of energy."

"Whoa," Duncan muttered. "That's too much information, even for me."

Katya gurgled and kicked her legs, drawing Jack's attention back to the baby. "You said fifty minutes, Dunk?"

"Right." He looked around. "Man, did something die in here?"

"The kid dropped a full load," Tyler said.

"It's going to be a long chopper ride if no one cleans that up."

Jack held Katya toward Duncan. "Nice of you to volunteer."

"Forget it."

"Don't look at me," Tyler said quickly. "I wouldn't know where to start."

Jack glanced at Eva again. The easiest course of action would be to wake her up so that she could change Katya's diaper, but he didn't want to do that. She was going to need all the strength she could manage once they got out of here. He nodded his chin toward the pack where he'd stored the baby's supplies. "Come on, guys, how hard could it be?"

The orchard was in bloom. The sight of the blossoms drew Eva forward, through the hay field to the split rail fence. She climbed over the top rail and lifted her face to the breeze. This was how home felt. It must be close.

Eva tumbled to the ground on the other side of the fence and ran between the rows of trees. Petals drifted past her face like velvet snowflakes. She spread her arms and turned up her palms to catch them. She wanted to show them to Grandma. She'd been away so long and couldn't wait to get home.

Voices drifted with the petals. Men's voices. Her feet slowed. The ground turned soft, pulling her feet deeper with each step until she could no longer run. She fell to her knees and started to crawl, but her hands slipped on the carpet of petals and her face hit the ground. She spread her fingers and stretched forward. Just a bit farther. Only a little bit more. She was so close....

A baby was crying somewhere among the trees. Eva stopped and looked behind her but saw only blackness. Where was the baby?

Now she smelled pine needles, not apple blossoms. The ground was scratchy beneath her cheek and cold stone slid beneath her fingertips.

Stone. The tower floor. Eva came awake with a start, her heart pounding. She pulled her hand back on the pallet and spread her fingers over the empty blanket. *Katya.*

The baby wasn't crying. She was making the cooing gurgle that meant she was happy. Eva could hear Jack's voice, as well as the voices of the other members of the team. They were speaking too quietly for her to make out their words. There didn't seem to be any urgency in their tone.

She braced her hand beneath her and sat up. The men were standing in a group just inside the doorway. She blinked a few times until her eyes adjusted and she was able to recognize Jack's silhouette against the starlit sky. He was holding the baby tucked to his side like a football.

She raked her hair off her face, not surprised to notice that her hands were shaking. She wasn't accustomed to waking up without being in reach of her daughter.

Why had Jack taken her? The moonlight overhead gave enough illumination for her to see that he'd left his rifle beside the pallet. His coat was spread out on the floor, and his pack was on its side with baby clothes strewn around it, as if he'd been searching for something.

Of course, she knew he hadn't been looking for the disk. He knew where it was. She touched the front of her coat and traced the outline of the case. The memory of what she'd said to him earlier washed over her, along with a wave of remorse. Her accusations had been unfair. She should have realized that Jack wasn't like Burian at all.

A man doesn't need an ulterior motive to want to touch you.

But he'd done more than touch her. He'd kissed her.

Eva rolled to her feet, impatient with herself. She had to stop thinking about that kiss. It had been wrong, a temporary lapse in judgment that wouldn't be repeated. There were far more important things to worry about. She moved toward the doorway.

"She dropped the mitten again," Matheson said, bending down to pick it up.

"You need to tie that ribbon tighter," Jack said.

"No way this hat's staying on," Colbert muttered, leaning over Katya. "There's no place to tie the ribbon. The kid's got no chin."

"One of those snaps on her slippery thing came open."

"It's called a snowsuit."

"Whatever." Matheson pushed at Jack's shoulder. "Lift her up so I can reach it."

Jack shifted Katya to both hands and held her up so that she dangled in front of him. She obviously liked the change in position because she started kicking her feet.

Matheson made a grab for her leg and missed. "Don't let her do that. She'll wriggle out of another diaper."

"Yeah, if that happens you're on your own, Jack," Colbert said. "I'm not getting near one of those things again. This was already above and beyond the call of duty."

Eva stared, torn between shock and amusement. The coat on the floor, the scattered baby supplies…it didn't take a genius to add that up. It seemed that for some reason the men must have decided to change Katya's diaper themselves.

They were commandos, trained to handle deadly weapons with ease. The more dangerous the situation, the more competent they seemed to become. They were so quintessentially male that it was difficult to picture them undertaking a task that was so, well, tame.

She wished she'd been awake to see it. "Do you want me to take her now?"

Jack spun toward her so quickly that Katya's legs flew sideways. She squealed with pleasure.

Colbert stretched his arm and put his hand over her mouth. "Keep her quiet, Jack."

Any amusement Eva had felt flipped to outrage. She stepped forward and shoved at Colbert. He was too solid for her to budge, but he did lift his hand from Katya. "What do you think you're doing?" she demanded. "Are you trying to smother her?"

Jack turned to place himself between her and Colbert. "Eva, we wouldn't hurt her."

"It's for everyone's safety, ma'am," Colbert said. "Your child can get loud when she cries. We can't let her give away our position."

Eva took a few deep breaths and bit back her protest. Her reaction had been instinctive, not logical. None of these men would deliberately try to harm Katya. In her brain, she knew that. They'd just been taking care of the baby. As Jack kept telling her, they were on her side. And Colbert was right. They couldn't let Katya cry.

"I understand," she said, striving to sound reasonable, "but muffling her like that wouldn't quiet her. It would probably only upset her more."

Jack pulled the baby against his chest and patted her back. "She wasn't crying, anyway. That's one of her happy sounds."

The other two men exchanged looks. "Sounds as if he knows more than he let on," Matheson said.

Colbert nodded. "What did I tell you? It's those dolls. Effective conditioning tools."

"Guys…"

"Maybe you could sing her a lullaby, Father Goose."

"Nah," Matheson said. "Don't you remember that karaoke bar in Yokohama?"

"Right," Colbert said, ducking his head to step through the doorway. "Hearing Jack sing would make the kid screech for sure."

Matheson followed. Gonzales' and Lang's voices came from the shadows outside the tower. The men spoke briefly, but as before, they pitched their voices too low for Eva to make out their words.

Jack cleared his throat. "Good news. Our evac is on its way."

He'd spoken so matter-of-factly that it took a second for his words to sink in. When they did, the relief was so strong her knees buckled. She slapped her hand against the wall for support. Thank God, it was almost over.

She looked outside, but she could see nothing in the sky except stars. She couldn't hear anything, either.

"That's why we figured we'd better, uh, change the baby."

She returned her attention to Jack and smiled. "Thank you. Katya hates being wet. It was really nice of you. I would have done it myself except I must have dozed off."

"How are you feeling?"

"Better now. You're sure the helicopter is on its way?"

"That's what Duncan heard. He'll keep us updated on the ETA. It won't be long."

Eva touched her fingertips to Katya's back. "I'm sorry I jumped on him about muffling Katya. I know he wouldn't try to hurt her. It just seems that my emotions keep overruling my reason lately."

"Stress can do that."

"And I do want to apologize for what happened earlier."

"What?"

"About the disk. My accusations were unfair."

"I thought we already cleared that up."

"We didn't really get the chance to talk."

"Right. Our tongues got in the way."

Instantly, the feelings he'd stirred with his kiss returned. It didn't matter that the other guys were only a few steps away or that the end of the journey was finally in sight. She wanted to step into his arms. She wanted to feel his warmth and his strength, taste the fresh tang of his lips, have her body come alive again….

Eva took Katya from him and stepped back. "We both agreed that kiss was a mistake."

"Yeah, we did, didn't we?" He raked his hands

through his hair. Then he moved past her to where he'd left his pack. He knelt and began to gather the baby supplies that were scattered on the floor. "Adrenaline wears off. So does the attraction. That's what the shrinks say."

"You told me you'd seen it happen before."

"A few times."

"To you?"

Even in the dimness she could see his jaw tighten. "Not to me," he said. "It involved some former members of the team you haven't met. They ended up jeopardizing the missions. They could have trashed their careers."

"What happened?"

"They sorted it out in time, and we got through it."

"But they're not in Eagle Squadron anymore?"

"No. Sarah took a job at headquarters. Rafe started up a security contractor business. I told you about them yesterday. Flynn left to join Rafe's company a month ago." He stuffed a handful of baby clothes into his pack. "So they gave up their careers in the end anyway."

She watched his body flex as he stretched to reach for a stray sock. And she reminded herself yet again that the attraction was only temporary. She held Katya to her shoulder with one hand and leaned over to pick up a tiny undershirt. "Here, you missed this." Her fingers brushed Jack's as she handed it to him.

He captured her hand. "What did you see in Burian?"

Her skin tingled from the contact with his. Touching Burian had never caused this kind of reaction. But it was bound to wear off. "We had many things in common."

"You mean your work."

"Primarily, yes. And I admired him."

"He's old enough to be your father."

"It hadn't mattered. I believed I was in love." She tugged her hand free, then sat cross-legged on the blanket so she could hold Katya on her lap. "Have you ever been in love, Jack?"

"No way. Norton men don't do love."

"What does that mean?"

"I told you. I come from a long line of gamblers and soldiers. No room for mushy stuff in my life."

"Don't you have a girlfriend?"

"Not currently. Why?"

"You keep asking *me* about my personal life. Why shouldn't I know about yours?"

"There's nothing to tell." He fastened his pack with a few sharp tugs. Then he sat back on his heels to face her. "I'm single and plan to stay that way. And like I said, you already met most of my family."

"What about your parents? What are they like? Where do they live?"

"My mother died when I was fourteen. My father was AWOL for most of my childhood and disappeared for good before my mother's funeral. I don't know where he is."

"I can see why your home with the army means so much to you."

"Like I said, it's what I do."

"You also said you drifted around before you enlisted?"

"From foster homes to juvenile detention centers." His teeth gleamed as he gave her a smile. "I used to steal cars then, too."

"But you turned your life around."

"That was thanks to my probation officer. He got fed up when I turned eighteen and introduced me to an army recruiter. End of story."

She didn't think so. As before when he'd spoken of himself, Jack had given her the bare minimum of information, but there had been a wealth of hurt in those terse sentences. Despite his ready humor and his easygoing manner, she could see there was much more to him than he wanted people to think. She remembered what she'd thought the first time she'd gotten a good look at his face. He'd seemed like a rebellious boy behind the mask of a man. She realized that she'd been right, but she hadn't guessed the reason.

He'd grown up without a father, just as she'd grown up without a mother. Had he felt the emptiness, too? She'd tried to fill hers by excelling at school. That was the only way she'd earned her father's attention. Had Jack tried to fill the void with recklessness and rebellion? It fit. It explained why he felt he needed to deny any tenderness inside him. She'd done the same thing, until Katya had come along. She wished she could know him better. If only they had more time...

What was she thinking? Their association would end when he got her to safety. As far as she was concerned, that couldn't happen soon enough.

A shadow blocked the starlight in the doorway. Jack grabbed his rifle and pushed himself to his feet just as Matheson spoke from the threshold. "Heads up, Jack. We've got incoming."

Jack went to look outside. "Is it the chopper?"

"One of them is. There's something approaching from the road, too."

Eva held her breath. For a moment she could hear nothing but the pounding of the pulse in her ears. Gradually she became aware of a distant throb, like the beat of a helicopter. Clutching Katya to her shoulder, she rose from the pallet and moved to the doorway in order to peer past Jack.

The sky was still empty. There was no sign of any of the other men on the moonlit hillside, but a pinpoint of light shone near the road she and Jack had followed to get here. "Oh, my God," she breathed, staring as the light resolved into twin beams. "It can't be Burian's men, can it?"

"Junior?" Jack asked.

"Duncan hasn't heard any word about pursuit."

"That didn't mean much before. Looks like they did get a message off about Eva not being on the truck. Where did Kurt leave it?"

"On the far side of where those lights are."

"Damn. Could they have followed you?"

"No. If it's someone from the complex, then they figured it out on their own."

"I can see how. Once they knew you were a decoy, they'd start looking in the opposite direction. Since we decided this would make a good rendezvous point, they could have, too."

"The guys are already digging in. We'll make our stand here."

Eva looked from one man to the other. "Stand?" she repeated. "No, we have to leave. We can take the car. We can't stay here and wait for them to find us!"

"It's okay, Eva." Jack slipped his arm behind her shoulders. "This is a defensible position, and the walls of this tower are thick enough to stop anything short of a mortar. With evac so close, we're better off staying put."

"Don't worry, ma'am," Matheson said, turning away. "I've got a few tricks that will slow down any party crashers."

She craned her neck to watch him go, but he soon disappeared against the hillside. She studied the lights on the road. Were they getting nearer?

"It might not be Burian's men," Jack said.

"Who else would it be?"

"It might be nothing but a guy who got lost coming home from market day or a pair of teenagers looking for a place to make out." He drew her away from the doorway. "But just in case it isn't, you'd better give me the baby. I'll carry her."

"I can do it. My wound's healing well. You saw that for yourself."

He stroked a lock of hair from her cheek. "Believe me, I haven't forgotten what I saw." He pressed the pad of his thumb to her lower lip. "Or tasted."

It was more than a tingle that she felt this time. It was a sexual jolt that traveled to every nerve in her body.

Was she insane? How could she feel anything at all beyond fear? "Jack…"

"Sorry," he muttered, dropping his hand. He returned to the pallet and spread the carrier on the blanket.

She took a few bracing lungfuls of fresh air before she followed him.

"Your wound isn't the only reason I should carry Katya," Jack said. "I'm stronger than you. When we go, we'll want to move fast, and her weight won't slow me down."

He was right. His physical strength and stamina were far greater than Eva's. He would be able to protect her daughter better than she could. As much as she longed to keep Katya right where she was for her own comfort, she knelt beside Jack to slide the baby into the pouch on the carrier. Together they managed to get the straps tied around him, despite the trembling in her hands.

Her emotions really were a mess. It was bad enough that she couldn't control her physical reaction to Jack. The warmth that coursed through her as she watched him cup his palm over Katya's back and rise to his feet had nothing to do with sex. It came from her heart.

A day ago she wouldn't have trusted him with the disk. Why, then, was she willing to trust him with the most precious piece of her world?

Jack drew on his coat over Katya and then clasped Eva's hand and guided her to stand beside him with her back to the wall. The thrum of the helicopter's engine was unmistakable now. She could feel the vibrations travel from the stone floor through the soles of her boots. It had to be close. Maybe it would reach them before—

Any hope of getting away cleanly was shattered in the next instant. Gunfire erupted from the hillside.

Eva cringed and moved closer to Jack. Beyond his shoulder she saw light glare from the sky. It was a spotlight from the helicopter, she realized. It moved across the slope, sweeping over rocks and white swaths of snow until it steadied on a distinctive blue vehicle. One of the complex's SUVs was partway up the hill. Its doors were open.

Burian's men were here. Outside. She could see dark shapes moving in the spotlight. "Jack!" she cried.

The aircraft was directly overhead now. He had to shout to be heard over the din of its engine. "Our ride's here. We move as soon as it lands."

It sounded to her as if Burian had brought an army. The rattle of gunfire was unrelenting. "We'll be shot!"

"The guys will keep them busy. We'll be fine." He squeezed her hand and released her. "Keep your head down and stay with me. Ready?"

Her heart felt as if it were going to beat out of her body. It was worse than the other times they'd been under fire, far worse, because the end was so close. "Ready!"

Rock, dirt and snow exploded from the hillside. Another explosion turned the SUV into a fireball. The flames reflected from the windshield of the helicopter as its landing skids touched the ground.

Jack propelled her from the doorway. "Now!"

Eva ran. Within three strides, the other commandos appeared from the darkness beyond the spotlight to provide a moving escort for her and Jack. While Matheson lobbed one grenade after another at Burian's troops, the rest of the men laid down a barrage of covering fire. Though Eva expected to feel the agony of another bullet striking her flesh at any second, before the fear could take hold, the helicopter was in front of her and hands were lifting her through the open door in the fuselage.

The rest was a blur. Except the sound of Katya's sleepy wails. And the warmth of Jack's embrace. Eva pressed her face to his shoulder and, with her daughter, shared the shelter of his arms.

Chapter 8

Dawn was already lightening the sky when Eva felt a gentle nudge against her leg. She turned her head and saw that Jack was smiling at her. For a moment she thought she must be dreaming. The night had been endless. There had been little to smile about. But then he pressed his leg against hers again and put his mouth next to her ear so that she could hear him over the noise of the helicopter's engine. When his breath warmed her skin, she knew she must be awake. "Look there," he said, extending his arm past her.

She followed the direction he was pointing. She and the team were sitting on metal benches that ran lengthwise along the helicopter's fuselage. Through the narrow opening to the cockpit, she could see only water and sky past the windshield. They had stopped briefly to refuel on a navy frigate in the Black Sea several hours ago, so she guessed they were now over the Mediterranean. Was that what he had wanted to show her? She glanced back at Jack. "What?" she mouthed.

He pointed again, this time lowering his head to align his cheek with hers to help her see what he did.

She tried once more, squinting past the silhouettes of the pilots. This time she saw a dark, gray shape on the water that looked like a small island. It was long and oddly flat, except for a squared off area in the center....

It wasn't an island. It was a ship. The sheer size of it had misled her. This must be the aircraft carrier Jack had told her they were heading for. Though it was at the limit of the helicopter's flight range, it looked as if they were really going to make it.

He put his lips to her ear again. "Almost there, Eva."

Yes, the nightmare was nearly over. Safety was within sight, within reach. She wanted to smile and shout with triumph, but all she could manage was a brisk nod.

She looked at the men who sat across from her. Lang was slumped on the bench, his eyes closed and his chin on his chest. Gonzales' eyes were closed, too, only he slept with his head tipped back against the fuselage and his mouth open. Matheson was rubbing a cloth over the stock of his rifle, but his movements were slow enough that he could have been doing it in his sleep. She turned her head to look past Jack and saw that Colbert appeared to be dozing, too.

They'd all more than earned a rest. Though she'd been too panicked to absorb many of the details about their escape from that hilltop, she remembered enough to appreciate how well the team had worked together. Truly like brothers.

And like a real family, there was a family resemblance.

Jack appeared as exhausted as the other men. His hair was standing up in furrowed tufts. The skin beneath his eyes was bruised with fatigue. Days worth of beard stubble darkened his jaw. As she watched him, his head tipped forward. He wasn't falling asleep, though. He was checking on Katya.

The baby was stirring in her carrier. She waved her bare fist in the air near Jack's chin. Her mittens had come off again sometime during the night, and he had been trying, in his own endearingly awkward way, to keep her hands tucked inside his coat.

Mere hours ago he'd been shielding her from stray bullets. Now he was just as determined to protect her from the cold.

Eva could feel the burn of tears in her eyes. She understood she was tired and overly emotional—and in no condition to regard Jack rationally. She really hadn't known him that long. Gratitude and relief were clouding her judgment. These were exceptional circumstances, and yet...

And yet she couldn't think of ever seeing a man look more attractive to her than Jack did at this moment. It wasn't simply due to his handsome features. It was the kindness beneath them. There was a fascinating contrast between his physical strength and his capacity for tenderness. Then there was his determination to fulfill his duty, his loyalty to his teammates and his sense of honor. He was a man who took his commitments seriously. Yet he'd said he planned to stay single. That was a shame, because he was the kind of man any woman could easily fall in love with.

He took Katya's hand and guided it beneath the edge of his coat. She pulled free and grasped his index finger. He looked surprised at first. Then he wiggled his finger within Katya's grip, his mouth quirking in a lopsided smile.

Oh, yes. Any woman could far too easily fall in love with Jack Norton.

The tears simply overflowed. There was nothing Eva could do about them. Too many days of fear, too many hours of running on hope and adrenaline, had left her raw. She and her daughter were on the verge of starting their new life. Jack would return to the work he loved. They were each getting what they wanted, so she had no reason to be sad.

Jack looked up and saw Eva's face. He touched his free hand to a tear on her cheek, his smile fading. "What's wrong?

"Nothing. I always cry when I'm happy."

"So, the operation went according to plan, Sergeant Lang?"

"Yes, sir. Except for the weather delay, everything went smoothly."

Apart from a slight lift of one eyebrow, Major Mitchell Redinger showed no reaction. As the commanding officer of Eagle Squadron, he was accustomed to his men's fondness for understatement. The details would come later during the debriefing, when they had more time and privacy. For now, like a father who had been waiting up all night for his wayward teenagers to return, he was seeing for himself that they had come through unscathed. He nodded his chin toward the helicopter that sat on the hangar deck behind them. The maintenance crew was already busy swarming around it, checking for damage. "And what about the bullet holes I noticed in the belly of that Seahawk?"

"Ryazan's men tried to persuade us not to leave, sir," Tyler offered.

"Are you certain they weren't Russian troops?"

"They weren't, sir," Colbert said. "Dr. Petrova identified them as guards from the complex. I later picked up some communications that confirmed it."

"It's odd that Ryazan didn't ask his government for help," Redinger said, "but that does leave things tidier for the diplomats. What about the extra passenger, Sergeant Norton? Any problems working the baby into the plan?"

Jack heard someone cough, but he kept his attention on the major's face. "Not at all, Major Redinger. Although, in the future…"

"Speak up, Sergeant. If you have a suggestion, I'd like to hear it."

"It wouldn't hurt the rest of team to learn the fundamentals of infant care, just in case this happens again."

"That's an excellent suggestion, Norton. We need to plan for every contingency. By the way, what's that on your boots?"

He glanced at the crusty white splotches that covered his toes. The milk that Katya had spat up had dried like epoxy. "Friendly fire, sir."

The major didn't smile often. Many people who didn't know him might suspect his craggy face had been carved from granite. Because of his rank, army protocol prevented him from fraternizing with the enlisted men who made up the team, yet there was no mistaking the sparkle of mirth in his steel-gray eyes. "Go get cleaned up and then get some rest. All of you." He paused. "And by the way, well done, men."

They saluted and picked up their gear. Jack shouldered

his pack, but he didn't head into the ship with the rest of the team. Eva and Katya were somewhere in this labyrinth. They had been whisked away by a pair of government people as soon as the helicopter had landed. He hadn't even had the chance to say goodbye.

It was what he'd expected. From this point on, what happened to Eva and her daughter was no longer Jack's concern. His involvement in their lives was finished.

"Was there something you wanted, Sergeant?" Redinger asked.

"Yes, sir. I'm concerned about Dr. Petrova's health. I'd like to make sure she's getting medical attention."

"I understand she was grazed by a bullet. Was it serious?"

"Not on its own. She appeared to be suffering from exhaustion as well."

"I'll ask her handlers to make sure she visits the infirmary."

"I'd appreciate it if you tell them she's in a fragile emotional state, too. Because of the stress."

"They've had experience with this kind of situation before, Norton. They'll know how to reassure her."

"Thank you, sir. There's one more thing."

"Yes?"

"There are extra clothes and diapers for the baby in my pack. She'll be needing them soon."

"I'll see that she gets them," Redinger said, holding out his hand for the knapsack.

Jack realized he was on the brink of refusing. He wanted to deliver Katya's things to Eva in person so he could be sure she was all right. The government people would be more interested in the information she brought than in her. They wouldn't have been prepared to deal with her daughter, either. Eva might try to put up a good front at first with that ice-princess act of hers, but he knew how emotional she could get. He hated to think of her anxious and alone.

"Is there a problem, Sergeant?"

"I still have my gear in there."

"I believe I'll be able to tell what belongs to you and what belongs to the baby, Norton."

He handed over the pack. "What's going to happen to Dr. Petrova now, Major?"

"That's not up to us. Your job's over." He regarded Jack more closely. "Or do I need to remind you?"

Jack assured him that he didn't.

After seventeen years in the army, it was the first time he'd out-and-out lied to a commanding officer.

The shower had been bliss. So had been putting on clean clothes. Eva didn't care that the T-shirt and pants were plain navy issue, or that the shower had been cramped and quick in the quarters that were on loan to her from one of the ship's officers. After the past few days, simply having running water had been an incredible luxury.

Katya had been happy to get clean, too, though she'd had to be content with a sponge bath. She had clean clothes as well, thanks to a tall, distinguished-looking man in an army uniform who had brought her the baby supplies that Jack had been carrying in his pack. And if Eva had been disappointed that Jack hadn't brought them himself, she'd done her best to get over it. She knew he would have other things to do now that his mission was over. He had other priorities, as did she.

Eva settled Katya more comfortably on her lap and focused her attention on the two other occupants of the windowless briefing room they'd been brought to. Meg

Hurlbut was a small woman, with neat gray hair and the kind of energy that made her seem taller than she was. Tim Shires appeared several years younger than her and spoke little, though his eyes were sharply assessing. The pair were from the Central Intelligence Agency. They'd shown her their identification, and the fact that they were here and had the cooperation of the ship's officers proved they must be who they said they were.

"How are you feeling now, Dr. Petrova?" Hurlbut asked.

It was more than a polite question, Eva thought. She'd been all but ordered to get checked out by one of the ship's doctors shortly after they'd arrived. "Much better, thank you."

"And your daughter?"

"She's in excellent health."

"She does appear to have come through her ordeal well."

Eva curled her hand over Katya's chest. "Yes, thanks to the men who helped us escape. They are outstanding soldiers."

"Eagle Squadron is reputed to be among the best units of our Special Forces," Hurlbut said. "Their commanding officer gave us a summary of the mission. It sounds as if they performed admirably."

The room shook with a booming thud. Eva started, as did the others, although the noise had been occurring at regular intervals throughout the day. She'd been told it was the sound of one of the catapults on the flight deck as it flung another plane into the air. "I hope you can pass on my appreciation to the team," she said. "I didn't get the chance to thank them properly when we arrived on the ship this morning. Or have they left already?" she added.

"I'm not sure." She glanced at Shires. "Any idea, Tim?"

"They keep their own schedule. My guess is they're already gone."

The catapult thudded again. The noise didn't appear to upset Katya. It shouldn't bother Eva, either, even though it meant another plane was leaving. Jack and the team could have been on any of them.

"Your escort must have been, ah, surprised to discover you had a baby with you," Hurlbut said.

"They adapted to the circumstances very well."

"It would have been easier for everyone if you'd alerted us to her existence beforehand," Shires said.

Eva held Katya more tightly. "It shouldn't make any difference to our bargain."

"It doesn't. We reached our agreement on the strength of the data that you sent your initial contact. It's been thoroughly analyzed, and your credibility is beyond doubt. Have you brought the proof you promised?"

"Yes. Are you prepared to provide asylum for both of us?"

"Certainly," Shires said.

"I personally guarantee it," Hurlbut added.

"What about possible custody issues that might arise with my daughter?"

"You were born in America, Dr. Petrova. Regardless of where your daughter was born, that makes her an American, as well. I will bring all the power of my agency to ensure she remains with her mother."

This was what she wanted to hear. Still, spoken promises were easily broken. "I don't mean to offend you, Ms. Hurlbut, but you're asking me to risk my daughter's future on the strength of your word alone."

Hurlbut nodded to Shires, who withdrew a folded sheaf of papers from inside his jacket. He spread them on the table so that they faced Eva. "These documents detail everything we have discussed concerning our obligations to you," he said. "We acknowledge that our country is in your debt. We fully intend to honor our agreement, Dr. Petrova. You don't have only our word as individuals, you have the guarantee of the United States Government."

It was more than she'd expected. Her hand shook as she drew the documents toward her. The print kept blurring, but she made herself read everything. It was as Shires had said. They'd committed their promises to paper. They'd even taken the time to add extra clauses that included Katya.

She looked at Hurlbut and then at Shires. They accepted her scrutiny without flinching. Having the promises in writing was no guarantee, either, yet could anything in life be one hundred percent certain? She'd been wrong to trust Burian, but she'd been right to trust Jack. Every instinct was telling her she could trust these people, too.

And being suspicious all the time was exhausting. Eva had done everything she could possibly do. She had anticipated this moment for weeks. Now that it was here, there was no turning back. It was the last bridge to cross. She took a few steadying breaths. Then she slipped her hand into the pocket of the pants she'd been given, withdrew the case with the disk and placed it on the table.

"The material I sent my contact was only preliminary research," she said. "This compact disk contains every detail that was on Burian Ryazan's computer as of three days ago concerning the biological weapon that the complex is developing. He's named it the Chameleon Virus."

"Why chameleon?" Hurlbut asked.

"Because it's a hybrid of a poison and a pathogen, part chemical agent and part biological, and thus exhibits properties of both. It also has the ability to adapt itself to its environment. It was developed on the framework of the virus that causes AIDS, but it manifests far more quickly. Its incubation period is days rather than months or years. Upon infection, it tailors itself to the host's DNA and begins to attack the body from within. The result is similar to congestive heart failure. The mortality rate of the Chameleon Virus is one hundred percent."

"How close to completion is the Chameleon program?" Hurlbut asked.

"If progress continues at its present rate, Burian will be able to mass produce the virus within sixty days."

They looked at her in silence for a moment. Eva was grateful for that. She needed time to let the taste of the words she'd spoken fade from her mouth.

It was Shires who was the first to move. He leaned forward and extended his arm across the table. "We appreciate your cooperation, Dr. Petrova."

Eva steepled her fingers over the case before he could take it. "When will my daughter and I be able to travel to America?"

"We'll start our trip home first thing tomorrow. However, we'd like to begin uploading the information from your disk as soon as possible."

Tomorrow. Less than twenty-four hours. Home. The farm, the apple orchard…

No, her home was gone. She would make a new one, just her and Katya.

"Dr. Petrova?"

The room was spinning. Eva jerked her head up and forced herself to focus. "I didn't have the time to review the data after I gathered it. It may be difficult to interpret."

"We have our country's top scientists standing by to analyze it," Hurlbut said. "We understand the urgency of the situation, and the captain is allowing us to use their secure uplink while we're on the ship. Time is of the essence if we want to prevent a tragedy."

"Furthermore, we need to leave our allies with no doubts as to the accuracy of our information," Shires put in. "They will want to be as certain as we are that our intelligence isn't flawed. It's the only way to get the international consensus we need."

"I would be willing to assist you in any way I can," Eva said. "I feel responsible for much of this. I had believed by unlocking the secrets of DNA production that we would find the key to conquering diseases like cancer that reprogram our DNA. During my first few years at the complex, we did produce drugs that are currently being used in cancer treatments."

Shires nodded. "It's why Ryazan's complex wasn't on anyone's watch list. And no doubt the income from those drug patents helped fund the Chameleon program."

Eva rubbed her forehead. "I had no clue I was contributing to the development of something that would kill."

"You've more than remedied that by coming forward."

"I only want the program to be stopped."

"We all do." Hurlbut scraped back her chair and rounded the table. The businesslike demeanor she'd maintained until now fell away as she leaned over to stroke Katya's hair. "I have a daughter, too," she said quietly. "And she has three children of her own. I don't want them to inherit a world where scientific breakthroughs are perverted to serve the ends of a handful of power-hungry men."

Shires shifted in his seat. "Meg, it's not only men—"

"Sorry, Tim, but it usually is." She smiled at Eva. "You're a courageous woman, Dr. Petrova. Someday your daughter is going to be very proud of what you've done."

Eva was uncomfortable with the praise. "All I want is for her to be safe."

"She already is," Shires said. "You both are." He swept his arm in a gesture meant to encompass more than the windowless room. "Though you're not yet on American soil, this vessel more than qualifies as American jurisdiction. It's a floating city, powered by two nuclear reactors, guarded by its own group of support ships, equipped with the most sophisticated detection and defense measures that are available. You are surrounded by thousands of trained sailors and aviators. I promise that you are perfectly safe."

"But if you wish to hold on to the disk until we get home," Hurlbut added, "that's your prerogative. We've arranged accommodation for you in Washington and will provide you with protection until this situation is resolved."

Eva laid her palm flat on the disk case as Hurlbut and Shires went on to detail their plans, both for the information she carried and for her and Katya. They had obviously given far more thought to what would come after her escape than Eva had. They hoped to have Burian's research stopped and the complex shut down through diplomatic pressure on the Russian government, but if that failed, they were prepared to take their case to the UN. Eva could be required to testify. After that, though, she would have the freedom of any other American citizen.

She could live where she wanted, work where she chose and raise Katya in an environment without fear.

Gradually, what they'd said began to sink in. This terrible knowledge was no longer Eva's burden alone to bear. It was theirs. She and Katya were indeed well beyond Burian's reach. His guards wouldn't be capable of getting to either of them now. With the help of the American government, Burian was going to be exposed as the evil man he was. His reputation was going to be ruined. No reputable scientist would be duped by him again.

Nor would an innocent, vulnerable young woman, fresh from a sheltered existence in academia and still grieving for her father...

How could she have believed that she'd once loved that monster?

Eva didn't want to keep this reminder of her mistake a moment longer. She shoved the disk across the table to Shires, wiped her hand on her pant leg and stood.

The meeting was over. The final bridge was burned.

It was time to get on with her life.

Chapter 9

Eva was feeling light-headed when she walked back to her quarters from dinner. She hadn't been able to eat more than a few bites. Whether her lack of appetite was from relief or fatigue, she didn't have the chance to figure out because the moment she turned down the final corridor she spotted Jack leaning against her door.

She had to blink to make sure she wasn't imagining him. She had been sure that he'd already left the ship, yet here he was, large as life, his arms folded on his chest and one ankle crossed comfortably over the other, as if he'd been waiting for some time. He turned his head at the sound of her footsteps, then straightened and smiled. "Hello, Eva."

She had to stifle the urge to run to him. She would have thought her emotions would be stabilizing by now. The effect that Jack had on her should be fading, too. She had no excuse to seek his arms. His mission was over.

But that didn't mean she couldn't drink in the sight of him as she walked closer. Oh, he looked better than any man should. He'd shaved, so there was no longer any beard stubble to blur the strong lines of his jaw. The clothes he'd worn for the past three days were gone, and he wore a clean set of fatigues. As she drew nearer, she caught the faint tang of soap and shampoo. His smile was making the laugh lines crinkle around his eyes and a dimple peek out beside his mouth.

Images flashed through her mind. Jack watching her in the moonlight, tense and unsmiling. Jack running down the road toward her with Katya strapped to his chest. And Jack cradling her face in his hands as he leaned down to kiss her.

"How are you doing?" he asked.

"Fine, thanks. And you?"

"Okay. Did you get something to eat?"

She looked at his mouth, and she remembered how he had tasted. She wasn't in danger any longer. Her accelerating pulse wasn't due to adrenaline. Yet she still wanted to feel his lips on hers. "Yes. The CIA agents saw to that."

"So the feds are treating you all right?"

"They're going through with our deal. I gave them the disk."

He studied her. "And you feel okay about it?"

"Definitely. They seem like decent people." She pressed her cheek to Katya's head. "We're leaving for Washington tomorrow."

"That's great."

"Yes, it's the start of our new life. What about you, Jack? Where do you go from here?"

He lifted one shoulder. "We're hitching a ride to the

nearest base tonight. From there we'll work our way back to Bragg."

"Where's that?"

"Fort Bragg's in North Carolina. It's not that far from DC. Maybe we can keep in touch."

Oh, yes. Please. Touch me. Eva saw his eyes darken. God, could she have said that aloud? He was just being polite. They were back in the real world, and this was a normal conversation. She had to control her emotions. "Yes, perhaps we could."

He leaned to the side so he could see Katya's face. "Looks like the squirt's asleep."

"It's been a long day for her."

"Yeah. Eva, I—"

"Jack, why are—"

They had spoken at the same time. There was an awkward silence. She hated it. After the intense days and nights they had shared, how could there be awkwardness between them? As if they were strangers?

He reached into the pocket of his pants. "I wanted to return these to you," he said, extending his hand to her.

She looked down. He had Katya's mittens on his palm. Against his large hand, they looked impossibly small.

"They were in my coat pocket," he said. "I'd forgotten I'd put them there while we were on the helicopter."

Another image blurred through her mind, one of Jack smiling as he let Katya grasp his finger.

"I know she doesn't keep them on that well," he said, "but I thought she might need them later."

The thought came out of nowhere. Why couldn't *he* have been Katya's father? Jack was everything that Burian wasn't. He was tender, considerate and protective. Why couldn't she have fallen in love with a man like Jack?

Eva slammed that mental door before she could examine the thought more closely. Jack had just been doing his job. How many times did she need to remind herself of that? She pressed her lips together so they wouldn't tremble as she took the mittens from his hand.

He closed his fingers over hers before she could draw away. "Are you really all right, Eva?"

The contact stole her breath, even though it was only their hands. He'd held her hand countless times already. This shouldn't be affecting her. "Of course. Why shouldn't I be? I'm getting everything I wanted." She tugged free and opened the door to the room she'd been given. She could feel the pressure of tears again, but she was determined to maintain her dignity so she averted her face. He'd seen her at her worst too often. "Excuse me. I need to put Katya to bed."

He followed her inside without waiting for an invitation, as if they were old friends, or maybe lovers….

She had to stop thinking like this or she was going to make a complete fool of herself.

There wasn't much space in the cabin, only enough room for a bed on one side and a small desk and set of drawers on the other, so he stayed by the door. She could feel his gaze on her as she laid Katya in the center of the bed and changed her diaper.

"You sure make that look easy," he said. "The guys and I took about a half hour."

"It's a matter of practice. My first attempts were probably no better than yours, and I had the advantage of books."

"Books?"

"Child care. I ordered dozens when I learned I was pregnant. I spent all my spare time studying how to be a mother." She used a rolled-up blanket as a bolster to keep Katya in place as she finished cleaning up. Once she assured herself Katya would remain asleep, she switched on the desk lamp and angled it so it wouldn't shine on the bed. She gestured to Jack to flick off the overhead light, then turned her back to take the documents Shires had given her from the waistband of her pants.

"What's that?" he asked.

She set the papers on the desk. "The CIA people put their promises in writing."

"That's impressive. They must really want what you have." His voice held a smile. "And I see you still haven't broken the habit of hiding things under your clothes."

She smoothed her shirt over her stomach self-consciously. "My hands were full with Katya. I had no other way to carry the papers."

"It's good you're not using that carrier for the kid. Your wound—"

"Is fine," she interrupted. "I already was examined by one of the doctors at the ship's infirmary. I carried my daughter in my arms because I wanted to hold her, that's all. Sometimes I just need to do that. She's too young to understand my words, but I'm sure she can feel the love in my touch. She needs love just as much as she needs warm clothes and a full stomach." She stopped short when she saw the odd look on his face.

"I bet you never learned that part from books," he said.

"I didn't have to learn to love Katya. It just happened."

"She's a lucky kid." He slipped his hands into his pockets and leaned his shoulders back against the door.

"These navy guys should have found you a bigger cabin. Or brought in an extra cot. Where are you going to sleep?"

"I can share the bed with Katya." She waved her hand in front of her. "It's only one night. Though I appreciate your concern, you don't need to worry about me any longer. I'm not your responsibility."

"I know that."

"Still, I am glad that I got the chance to see you again, Jack. I wanted to thank you for everything you did. I know words are inadequate, considering the danger you put yourself in for me, but I do want you to know how very grateful I am."

"I don't need your gratitude. It was my job, Eva."

"Yes, I'm fully aware of that. Please, tell the rest of the team that I appreciate their efforts, as well. You mentioned you're leaving tonight?"

"That's right."

"Then I imagine you must be eager to get going."

He looked from her to Katya. "Sure. I don't like staying in one place for long."

"Of course. Like your great-great something grandfather. If there was a riverboat, you'd be on it."

"Damn straight."

"And you must be eager to get started on your next mission. More danger and excitement."

"You bet."

"Lots of gunfire and exploding grenades and jumping out of trucks."

"Only if we're lucky."

She took a step forward and held out her hand. "Well, goodbye, Jack."

He hesitated and then pushed away from the door

and clasped her fingers. "Do you really want me to leave, Eva?"

She gave her hand a tug, but this time he held on. "Why are you asking me that? You said you're scheduled to move out tonight."

"That's tonight. I meant now. Do you want me to leave you alone?"

No, I want you to stay with me, with us. I don't want our time to end. Ever.

She had to lie. It would be best if she did. But he was standing close enough for her to feel the warmth from his body and catch the scent that rose from his skin. She was finding it more difficult by the second to form any kind of thought. "You said you only wanted to bring back Katya's mittens."

He bent his head to look at their joined hands. "That's what I tried to tell myself, but it's not the only reason I tracked you down."

"No?"

"I needed to see you again. To make sure you were all right."

"Well, you've done that. We're fine."

"Yeah." He rubbed his thumb over her knuckles. "That's great."

"Thank you. I appreciate—"

"Will you quit saying that?"

"What?"

"I don't deserve your gratitude, Eva."

"Of course you do."

He moved his head in a slow negative. "The truth is, what I really want to do right now is kiss you."

That's all he had to say, and her knees went weak. She swayed.

"Eva?" Jack released her hand and steadied her by the hips.

"You explained that to me already, Jack. What happened…in that tower was due to the circumstances. It was a temporary attraction."

"It didn't feel temporary. It felt damn good."

She put her hands on his chest. Through his shirt, she could feel the warmth of his skin. She imagined she could sense the beat of his heart, too. Or was it her own pulse? "But the mission's over."

"Exactly. That's the real reason I'm here."

"I don't understand."

"It's over, so that means I'm no longer a soldier who's duty-bound to protect you."

"Jack…"

He tipped up her chin with his index finger. There was no smile around his eyes now. His expression was intense as he searched her face. "I'm just a man who wants to kiss you."

Like the last time, Eva could have moved away. Jack would never force her to do anything. If she'd exerted the least amount of pressure on his chest, she was sure he would have released her and stepped back. It would be the sensible thing to do. Nothing could come of this, other than making saying goodbye even more difficult.

There were other thoughts, too. More protests from the cautious, logical part of her brain. As before, she didn't listen to any of them. Unlike the last time, though, she didn't wait for Jack to move first. She slid her hand to the back of his head, lifted on her toes and pressed her mouth to his.

This was what she'd needed, more than food, more than sleep. The feel of Jack's lips on hers, the taste of his mouth, the warmth of his breath, swept away her caution. There wasn't room for anything else.

Jack slid his fingers into her hair, holding her head steady as he deepened the kiss. She opened her mouth eagerly to take all that he would give her. Heat flowed to every intimate part of her body. And as the kiss went on, needs that had merely stirred the last time started to blossom.

It felt so simple, so right. Why had she tried to resist? He'd said he was just a man who wanted to kiss her. So for now, why couldn't she be just a woman who wanted him?

And she did want him. More than she could have dreamed.

She pressed closer. Her nipples tingled and hardened at the first contact with his chest. Pressure built in her breasts, but it wasn't from milk. It was from arousal. It had been so long. How could she have forgotten how good this felt?

Because it had never felt this good with Burian, she realized. Even being fully clothed, doing nothing but kissing, was sheer delight because this was Jack. She smiled against his mouth, looped her arms behind his neck and rubbed her nipples against his chest.

A groan rumbled through Jack's throat. He backed her the few steps to the desk and lifted her so she was sitting on the edge. He cupped her breasts through her shirt.

Pleasure crashed over her, pure and mind-numbing. She gasped.

"Sorry," he murmured, withdrawing his hands. "I know you're nursing. I didn't mean to hurt you."

"You didn't. It's just…" She grabbed his wrists

and returned his hands to her breasts. "They're very sensitive."

"Sore?"

"Not sore. Just the opposite. Really..."

He smiled. "Sensitive," he repeated, rotating the heels of his hands.

Her eyes half closed. "Mmm."

"Then it's okay for me to do this?" he asked, squeezing gently.

She could barely breathe. His caress felt so good. She nodded.

"What about this?" He stroked the undersides with his thumbs.

In reply, she reached for her buttons. She laughed when she saw her hands were too unsteady to manage them. "You'll need to help me, Jack."

He parted her shirt before she'd finished her request. It hit the floor, along with her nursing bra. Then he leaned over and pressed his face to the valley between her breasts. "I've wanted to do this for the longest time," he murmured. "You're so beautiful, Eva."

With his breath warming her skin, she did feel beautiful. Desired. Loved.

No, not that. Jack didn't do love.

But he knew how to make her body hum. He used his mouth and his hands and his voice, each caress building on the one before. The room swirled around her. She didn't see the gray steel walls. She didn't hear the faint clang of footsteps in the corridor or the distant throb of the ship's engines. She didn't think about the plane that would take Jack away tonight or the one she would board tomorrow. She didn't even think about her baby sleeping on the other side of the room. All she was conscious of was the pleasure that followed Jack's touch.

She slid off the desk and yanked at his shirt. He took it off more quickly than he'd gotten rid of hers. For a heartbeat she could only stare, her mouth going dry. He was magnificent. He had the build of an athlete, lean and powerfully muscled. She'd felt his strength so many times. Now she reveled in the freedom to look at him, to explore, to return the pleasure he was giving her.

The world contracted further, becoming a whirl of taste and texture and scent. With her hands and her lips, she learned the contours of the arms that had held her, the chest she'd sheltered against and the shoulders she'd leaned on while she'd slept. Time lost its meaning as sensations overwhelmed her. As naturally as breathing, she reached for the zipper of his pants.

Pleasure became urgency and then a driving, mindless need. They wasted no time ridding themselves of the rest of their clothes. Even if they could have used the bed, they wouldn't have made it there. She curled her foot behind his calf, trying to get closer. Jack slid his hands beneath her bottom and lifted her from the floor. Locking her ankles behind his waist, she hung on as he moved her. He was long and hard and, oh, he was pressing exactly where she needed him.

Eva trembled, her lips parting in shock. It was so fast. She couldn't possibly—

He shifted his grip and slipped one hand between her thighs.

Her climax was swift. Almost brutal. She turned her face to his neck to muffle her scream as her body convulsed.

"Eva?"

She gasped. She couldn't get enough air. The shudders tapered off to become shivers.

Jack lowered her to her feet. "Are you okay?"

She tried to reply. After what he'd so generously given her, she had to say something. But the instant her feet hit the floor, her legs buckled.

She was aware of Jack's arms around her and the concern in his voice. Then darkness closed in, and she felt nothing at all.

Jack held Katya to his shoulder as he paced outside the examining room. So far, the baby was still sleeping, but he could feel the telltale twitches she made that meant she'd be waking up soon. He paused at the door. He could hear nothing from inside. What the hell was taking them so long?

And what the hell had he been thinking? He'd known Eva was tired. He'd meant to stop with a kiss, that's all. But then he'd felt her response, and he couldn't have stopped if his life had depended on it.

Damn, he was a bastard. He'd known he would end up hurting her. Just not like this.

"Hey, Jack, what's going on? I heard you were trying to contact us."

At Tyler's voice, he pivoted and strode toward him. "Something's wrong with Eva. It's more than fatigue."

"The major wants us on the flight deck in an hour."

"Didn't you hear me? Eva's sick."

"Yeah, I heard you. They've got real doctors on this tub. They'll fix her up."

"They're worthless. They examined her this morning. They should have seen something was wrong, but they didn't." He looked past Tyler. "Where's Major Redinger now?"

"I don't know."

"What do you mean, you don't know? You just talked to him, didn't you?"

"That was a half hour ago. He'll meet us at the plane."

"We've got to take Eva to the hospital in Ramstein. Redinger can authorize the route change."

"If it's that serious, the ship's doctors will take care of the transfer. What did they say was wrong?"

"They didn't. They don't know anything. Someone should stuff their fancy medical degrees up their navy blue butts."

Tyler seized his arm. "What's the matter with you, Jack? Eva Petrova's not our problem anymore, remember?"

"Wrong. Our mission was to get her out safely."

"We did."

He jerked his arm free and swung it toward the door. "She's in there getting prodded and poked by a bunch of incompetent pill pushers. I don't call that safe."

At his raised voice, Katya bumped her head against his shoulder and started to cry. Jack returned his free hand to her back and jiggled her. "It's okay, squirt," he murmured, doing his best to sound calm. "Be good and go back to sleep."

Tyler crossed his arms and leaned one shoulder against a bulkhead, waiting until the baby had quieted. "How come you've got the kid anyway, Jack? I thought Eva was with the government spooks."

"I was the only one there when she collapsed."

"Where?"

"In her quarters. I called it in as a medical emergency, and they brought her down here. I couldn't leave the kid alone, so I took her with me. They won't let us in. They're not telling me anything, either."

"What were you doing in her quarters, Jack?"

"Returning the kid's mittens."

"Sure, you were."

Jack gritted his teeth. He'd told the doctors the truth about what had happened before Eva had lost consciousness because it might make a difference to their ability to come up with a diagnosis. He didn't want word of what he'd done to spread any further. "I'd found them in my coat pocket."

"Tell that to someone who doesn't know you, Jack. It's my guess what you were really doing had more to do with what was in your pants."

He jammed his forearm across Tyler's windpipe, clanging his head back against the bulkhead. "Careful, junior."

Tyler didn't blink. He could have easily countered the move. Jack had seen him in action, and he was larger and faster than Jack was. He wasn't hampered by the need to hang on to a baby with one arm, either. Instead, he slowly raised his palms.

Jack dropped his arm and stepped back.

Tyler rubbed his throat. "What the hell's wrong with you?"

"I don't want you talking about Eva like that. She deserves our respect."

"It's you I was talking about, not her."

Jack grunted. In the reasonable part of his brain, he realized his anger should have been directed at himself instead of his friend. But he'd been running on instinct from the time Eva had passed out, and he was feeling less reasonable by the second. "I'm worried about her, that's all."

"I can see that."

"She's a special woman. One in a million. She's made the most of everything that life's thrown at her and never gives up. She's a good mother, too. You've seen how she dotes on this kid. She deserves to be happy."

"You'll get no argument from me or any of the guys about that. She proved more than once that she's one brave lady."

"Not many people have her kind of courage."

"I could tell on the flight here that you two seemed pretty close."

"She relied on me. She counted on me."

"She's also a good-looking woman."

Jack shot him a warning glance.

"Just stating a fact, doc. I could see that you noticed."

"So?"

"So what you do on your downtime is your business, but you'd better get your head on straight in the next—" he glanced at his watch "—fifty-one minutes. The major won't wait."

Katya whimpered. Jack shifted her to a football carry and rocked her back and forth. "Tell Redinger I'm not going anywhere until I know Eva's all right."

Tyler scowled. "Think about this before you get carried away. Your head's still in the mission. You're confusing your sense of responsibility with genuine attraction. Eva's being taken care of. She doesn't need you."

"Don't quote the psych lectures to me, junior. I've heard them all. I've been going on missions since before you started to shave. Oh, I forgot. You're still not old enough to shave."

"Jack, I'm serious."

"So am I."

Tyler hesitated. "You can't mean that. You've only known her for a few days."

Jack raked his free hand through his hair and then squeezed the back of his neck. Was he mistaking adrenaline-induced desire for something more? He didn't think so. From the start, he'd been drawn to Eva on a level that went deeper than sex. The amount of time they'd had together didn't seem to matter—they'd connected as if they'd already recognized each other.

But he wasn't going to try explaining his feelings to Tyler. He wasn't sure he understood them himself.

The door to the examining room opened. A middle-aged doctor wearing wire-rimmed glasses and a set of scrubs that stretched over a weight lifter's build stepped out. He peered over his glasses first at Tyler and then at Jack. "Sergeant Norton?"

Jack didn't know him. He wasn't one of the doctors who had been on duty when they'd brought Eva here. How many physicians did she need? How bad was this? He stepped forward. "I'm Norton. How is she?"

"Dr. Petrova's awake and alert."

He exhaled hard. Had he overreacted? "Did you find out what's wrong?"

"We're not sure. We're waiting for some blood work."

"I need to see her," he said, starting past.

"Hold on, Sergeant. You can't do that."

Jack didn't slow down. "This is her daughter. Eva's probably been asking for her."

"She has, but until we know what we're dealing with, for the child's sake you should keep her away from her mother. We've moved Dr. Petrova into full isolation."

That stopped him in his tracks. He turned to face the doctor. "What the hell does that mean?"

"As I said, we're running some further blood tests."

"You know she's a nursing mother, right? And she's

been through a traumatic experience. The bullet wound in her side was cleansed, but—"

"Sergeant, I'm fully aware of Dr. Petrova's history. I've also been told of the circumstances that preceded her collapse," he added.

Jack met his regard levelly. "Good. Then you should understand that I'm not going to be placated with generalities. I'm going to stay in your face until you give me some real answers."

"Right now, all we know is there's something unusual in her blood."

"Is it an infection?"

"It appears to be some kind of virus, but so far we haven't been able to identify it. It's not like anything we've seen before."

A *virus?*

No. It wasn't possible. Eva worked at a computer, in an office. She didn't work in the complex's lab. She was too smart to have accidentally infected herself. Because of the baby, she would have been cautious to the point of paranoia.

Jack glanced past the doctor to where Tyler still stood in the corridor. He could see by the look on his face that his thoughts had followed the same path as Jack's.

Katya kicked her feet against his side. Jack moved her to his shoulder again and brushed his lips over her hair. Hair so like her mother's. Silky and fine. With a scent like honey. He held her tighter.

No! It had to be something else.

"As a precaution," the doctor continued, "I've been authorized to quarantine everyone who has come into contact with Dr. Petrova. Until we have some answers, no one is leaving this ship."

Chapter 10

The thick sheets of plastic that curtained Eva's hospital bed distorted the rest of the room into a colorless blur. Like the other rooms she'd seen on the ship, there were no windows. The hours crawled by with no distinction between day or night, only the steady beat of the heart monitor behind her to keep time. Beyond the door she could hear voices and the sound of people and equipment being moved, but the booming thud of the catapult on the flight deck had been silent from the time she'd woken up here more than two days ago.

She hadn't wanted Jack to leave, and he hadn't. She'd wished he could have stayed, and he had.

But she hadn't wanted him to stay because of this. Dear God, she'd thought the worst was over.

It was only beginning.

The signs had been there and growing worse since she'd left the complex—the fatigue, the dizziness, her inability to keep awake. The Chameleon Virus was beginning its assault on her body, but she hadn't wanted to admit it. She'd made excuses. She'd seen only what she'd wanted to see.

She'd done that with Burian and her research, too. She'd ignored the warning signs and had deceived herself into believing everything was fine, but she'd been wrong. And now because of her blindness she could have condemned Katya and Jack to death….

The room blurred. Eva forced herself to take deep breaths until her head cleared.

No! She wouldn't think like that. If it really was the Chameleon Virus that was causing her weakness, then Katya and Jack had to be all right. Burian had designed the virus to be stable when it was dormant—that was one of the aspects that made it such an easily deployed weapon. It adapted to an individual's DNA the moment it got into the host's body. Eva couldn't have passed it on to either of them.

At least, that's what she kept telling herself. She had to believe she wasn't mistaken about this. Otherwise, she would go insane.

The nurse who was drawing the latest blood sample patted Eva's arm. "All done." The lower half of her face was hidden behind a mask, but her brown eyes were filled with sympathy. She capped the vial and placed it in the rack she'd left on the tray table. "You should try to get some rest, Eva. Let this new medication do its job."

She pushed herself up on her elbows. The tube that snaked from her arm to the IV stand beside the bed rattled against the bed rail, along with the wire from the lead on her chest. She brushed them aside and sat up. "I can't rest. Where's my daughter now?"

"She's still in quarantine. She's being well looked after."

Eva glanced down at her breasts. They were hard, swollen globes under the hospital gown. Her body was demanding that she nurse Katya, but she wouldn't dream of endangering her child. During the last forty-eight hours, the doctors had pushed a cocktail of drugs into her system in an attempt to slow down the virus. She didn't want the drugs to filter through to Katya. And for all she knew, her milk could be poison. She could have been passing this horror to her daughter for days, just as her kiss had passed it to Jack....

No! She couldn't go there. They had to be all right.

She drew up her knees, wrapped her arms around her legs and pressed her aching breasts to her thighs. "Katya likes to be held. And she needs to be burped for at least fifteen minutes after she's been fed."

"Yes, we've all noticed your daughter is quite vocal about making her needs known."

"Is she still accepting the bottle?"

"She has too good an appetite to refuse it, but she pouts about it first."

Eva clenched her fists, trying to hold the tears at bay. The ship's doctors had consulted with pediatricians at a base hospital and devised an infant formula from the supplies available on board. Katya was getting nourishment; that's all that was important, even though the bottle Eva had packed among her baby supplies had been meant for water, not milk. She had planned to breast-feed her baby for a full year, just as the books had recommended.

But they weren't going to have a full year together. They might not have much more than a week. "How soon…" She stopped and swallowed hard. "How much longer before you know the results of the blood tests?"

The nurse placed her gloved hand over Eva's arm. "It should be soon."

"You'll tell me right away, won't you? I want to know. Either way. I *need* to know."

"The minute we learn anything about you or your daughter, we'll tell you. I promise."

"What about the soldiers who brought me to the ship? Are their results in yet?"

"We're processing everything as fast as we can, Eva. Have patience." She gave her arm a parting squeeze and then picked up the rack of blood samples and used her shoulder to push aside one of the plastic sheets. It settled back into place with a squeaking swish, leaving Eva alone.

That was the worst part of staying in this plastic-walled prison. This was the first time since she'd sensed her child's life growing within her that she'd been completely alone. She'd lived with emptiness before. She'd learned to fill it by using her mind, yet now that she'd opened her heart she could never go back to the way she'd been. Even if love hurt, she was going to embrace it.

Because in the end, it was only love that endured. Her own mother's face had grown hazy in her memory, but she remembered the love in her voice as she read from her book of fairy tales and the softness of her good-night kiss on her forehead. And there was the way Grandma's smile would crinkle all the lines on her face whenever Eva had taken her hand. Even her father had loved her in his own way. He hadn't been physically demonstrative, but his eyes had shone with love and pride with each award and degree she'd received. No matter what high-level diplomatic negotiations had been going on, he'd managed to be there for every one of her birthdays and graduation ceremonies except the last.

But Katya would be too young to remember anything. She wouldn't have the memory of her mother's touch to comfort her when she grew older. She wouldn't see the pride in her eyes. Eva wouldn't be there when her daughter graduated kindergarten. She wouldn't be there for her first birthday. She might not live to see Katya get off this ship.

And what would Jack remember about her? Would he think of her when he was finally free to leave? When he flew off to another mission, would he remember the passion they'd shared in that cramped, steel-walled cabin? And when he went home again would he meet some other woman who would be able to unlock all the tenderness he kept inside? He deserved to be happy, to have someone who loved him….

Eva dropped her forehead to her knees. The grief for what might have been was there, waiting to swallow her if she let it, but she wasn't going to give in. It would be a waste of the time she had left.

Dear God, she didn't want to die.

Plastic swished again. Eva lifted her head. Through her tears she saw that a man wearing the same kind of long-sleeved gown and mask as the nurses did was standing at the foot of her bed. "Are the test results in?" she asked.

"Not yet, Eva."

That was Jack's voice. She wiped her eyes fast and focused on what she could see of his face. "Jack? What are you doing here?"

"I was in the neighborhood and thought I'd drop by." He glanced at the monitor and the IV drip and then pushed aside the tray table and sat on the side of the bed. "How are you feeling?"

Her lips trembled. He was keeping his tone casual, just as he'd done when he'd first discovered her bullet wound. That seemed so long ago now. "Better than I was. With all the drugs they're giving me, I feel as if I shouldn't even be in this bed. What about you? Are you all right?"

"Other than getting stir crazy waiting around to hear from the doctors?"

"Yes, other than that."

"No fatigue, no dizziness. No sign that anything's wrong." He eased her arm away from her knees and took her hand. Even through the latex gloves he wore, his warmth flowed into her fingers. "Katya doesn't have any symptoms, either."

Hope surged. "You've seen Katya? She's really all right?"

"She's in the quarantine ward with us. So are those CIA agents and the helicopter crew."

"And the medical staff? They're treating Katya well?"

"She's got them all wrapped around her tiny fingers. Between Meg Hurlbut and the nurses, she gets enough attention for five kids. When she grows up she'll either have a great career as a drill sergeant or she'll have to look for a job opening for a princess. She sure seems to like being waited on."

He was trying to make her smile. That fact only brought a lump to her throat. "All I hope is that she does grow up."

"She will, Eva. She's strong, like her mother." He blotted her cheeks with the edge of the blanket. "You'll get through this."

"The Chameleon Virus is fatal, Jack."

"It might be something else. Someone could have coughed on those sausages we got in that town whose name I can't pronounce. It could be the flu. Or the mumps. Ever had the mumps?"

She gripped his hand. "I appreciate what you're trying to do, but we both know it's not the flu or the mumps."

"I'm not doing anything. I wish I could."

"Please, don't feel responsible for me. I know it was once your job to protect me, but this virus is one thing you can't protect me from."

He tipped back his head, his throat working. "I know."

"And I want you to know I never considered the possibility that I could have been infected. From the time I'd learned I was pregnant, I kept away from the laboratory building. I only went into Burian's lab the day before I left, but it's on the fourth floor. The containment levels are underground. That's where all the hazardous work is done."

"This isn't your fault, Eva."

She wished she could believe that. "I've gone over and over my actions, and I can't think of any other place I would have been exposed to the live virus. Even then, I don't know how it happened. The only thing I touched in Burian's lab was his computer. If I'd thought there was even a remote risk of contamination, I would have worn protective clothing."

"I know you would. You think everything through."

"And if I'd suspected what was wrong with me, I never would have kissed you. I'm sorry, Jack. I'm so sorry."

"Seems to me I was to blame for that, not you."

"No, I should have realized—"

"Will you quit apologizing? I make it a practice to do five dangerous things before breakfast, remember?"

Her laugh came out as a sob. She covered her face with her hands. The beeps from the monitor accelerated.

"Hey, that can't be good for you," he muttered. He lifted his arms to reach for her.

She straightened her legs and shoved herself farther toward the head of the bed. "No! You shouldn't be this close to me. Not until we know for sure what I've got."

"I had your blood on my skin a few hours after we met, and we've already shared bodily fluids. If I was going to get what you have, I'd already have it. I probably shouldn't bother wearing this mask."

"God, I'm sorry."

"Shh. Risk is part of my job." He leaned forward and laid his hands on her shoulders. "But making love to you wasn't. Eva, I let things get out of control. I hadn't meant for the kiss to go so far. I should have noticed that you weren't well, but I wasn't thinking. I'm the one who owes you an apology."

"Is that why you're here? Because you're sorry about what happened between us?"

"Hell, no. I'm apologizing for the way it ended. I'm not sorry it happened. Are you?"

She didn't have to think about her answer for one instant. "No. It felt wonderful."

"Except for the passing out part."

"Yes, except for that."

"The docs figure your increased pulse rate put too much strain on your heart. If I'd known—" he shook his head "—I don't think I would have stopped, Eva. I'm not that noble. Maybe I would have been gentler, but—"

"Jack, please. Don't feel guilty. It's a waste of time."

The word hung in the air between them. Jack rubbed

his thumbs across the cotton of her hospital gown. "It's not over yet."

"In another ten days—fourteen at the most—it will be."

"The spooks said they've got scientists back in the States who've been analyzing the data that was on the disk you gave them. Ted Shires brought his laptop into quarantine to follow their progress. They're sending e-mail updates to him and the medical staff here. Duncan's been keeping track of it, too. He told me the experts are learning more about the virus by the minute. They're bound to come up with something."

It was probably foolish of her, yet she wanted with every ounce of her being to believe him. And she wanted the comfort of his touch, his warmth, his familiar scent. But she couldn't touch him, and all she could smell was boiled cotton.

It didn't matter. His presence alone was like sunshine in the windowless room. He was a good man. A caring lover. She had plenty of regrets, but making love with Jack wasn't among them. She'd realized that one night would be all that they'd have even before she'd gotten sick. He'd given her more passion in a few hours than she'd known in her lifetime. He'd made her feel… alive.

Dammit, why did she have to meet him *now?*

"What are you doing here, Sergeant?"

Eva looked past Jack to the plastic curtains. Dr. Arguin, the doctor who had examined her most recently, had returned. He was frowning over his glasses at Jack.

And he wasn't wearing a mask.

Jack must have noticed it at the same time. He slid

from the bed and took a step toward the doctor. "What's going on? Did you lift the quarantine?"

"There's no reason to continue it."

"Then you got the test results? Eva's okay?"

Oh, yes, she thought. Please. Let it all be a false alarm. A bad dream. If they were lifting the quarantine, that meant they weren't worried she would spread anything.

But if it was good news, wouldn't the doctor be smiling?

"I'd like to speak to my patient alone, Sergeant Norton," he said.

Eva sat forward. "Please, don't make me wait any longer. Tell me now."

"Better do as she says, Doctor," Jack said, pulling off his own mask. "Because you should know I'm not going anywhere until you do."

Dr. Arguin moved to the foot of the bed. Instead of meeting Eva's eyes, he looked at the monitor and then down at his hands.

She could see the answer on his face before he spoke. She wanted to cover her ears to stop from hearing it. No. Oh, God, no!

"We've compared your blood samples to the latest data we received from the disk you provided," Dr. Arguin said. "I'm very sorry, Dr. Petrova. There's no longer any doubt. The pathogen in your blood is the Chameleon Virus."

Even though Jack had figured this was coming for the past two days, hearing the diagnosis confirmed was like a blow to the gut. He wanted to smash something. He wanted to swear. But the beat from the monitor was accelerating again, so for Eva's sake he could do neither. He turned and took her hand.

She laced her fingers with his and folded their joined hands to her breasts. He didn't think she realized she was doing it. Her attention was solely on the doctor.

"And my baby?" she asked.

"Your daughter is fine."

"Did you say—" Her voice broke. She pressed her lips together, her eyes brimming.

"There's no trace of the virus in her system, Dr. Petrova. We've taken blood samples at eight separate intervals over the past forty-eight hours, and they have all come back negative. Judging by the rate the virus multiplies, if it was present, it would have been detected."

She looked at Jack. Pain and joy warred on her face.

He pulled off his gloves and wiped a tear from her cheek. He could see that she was trying to retain control and it killed him. She was more concerned for her child than for herself. She had to be the strongest woman he'd ever met. "Katya will be fine, Eva."

She nodded. "And Sergeant Norton?" she asked. "The rest of the soldiers?"

"The same. All negative. It's as you said. The virus appears to have adapted itself to your DNA immediately."

"Then it's not contagious?" Jack asked.

"According to the experts, Dr. Petrova couldn't transmit it now any more than she could spread her eye color to someone else. This virus is unique, unlike anything I've seen before. It's behaving more like a poison than a microorganism."

"That's how Burian said he'd designed it," Eva

said. Her voice trembled. "To eliminate only the target population. A humane weapon that delivers a merciful death. He was very proud of what he'd accomplished." She closed her eyes. Her chest heaved with a sob.

Jack put his knee on the bed. Taking care not to dislodge Eva's IV tube or the monitor wire, he slipped his arms around her back and drew her toward him.

She didn't resist this time. She fitted her head into the hollow of his neck, just as she had so many times before. But this time, he couldn't shield her. He couldn't fight this enemy for her. He couldn't help her with some field first aid and a med kit, either. He'd never felt more useless in his life.

No, that wasn't right. This was how he'd felt when he'd watched his mother die. It had taken her years.

Eva had mere days.

The urge to smash something grew stronger. But that was okay. As he'd learned before, anger was easier to deal with than grief. That's why he'd blamed his father for his mother's death. He'd carried that rage around for years. He'd blamed himself, too, for not being able to help her. And some of the anger had been for his mother, because she'd given up, because she'd left him.

But there was no focus for his anger now, no one to blame other than fate.

He looked at the doctor. "Now that you know what Eva has, you can do something to help her, right?"

"We'll continue with the drugs we've been using. They appear to reduce the rate by which the virus is replicating itself."

"You mean you can slow it down?"

"To some extent."

Another ten days, fourteen at the most. He tightened

his arms around Eva. He could feel her shaking. Or was that him?

"Time to go, Sergeant. I need to examine my patient."

Eva raised her head. "Wait. Jack, I need to ask you something."

"Name it, Eva."

"I know it's not your responsibility, but I know I can trust you."

"Whatever I can do, I will."

"I need to know that Katya will be all right after…" Her voice cracked. "When I'm gone."

He didn't want to hear this. Not now. Not yet. She still could have another two weeks. But he knew she had to say it. That's the kind of woman she was. Her first concern would never be for herself. He clenched his jaw and nodded once.

"My mother had cousins in Ohio," she continued, her words coming quickly, as if she worried she wouldn't get them all out. "I didn't know them, but I remember they came to her funeral. Could you find them? See what kind of people they are? I want Katya to be raised by family."

Jack had been fourteen when the social service worker had removed him from the house. He'd had plenty of relatives, but none of them had been willing to take in a troublemaker like him. His memories of the first foster home were hazy. He wished he could forget the rest. He couldn't picture Eva's baby following the same path. "I'll find them," he said.

"And if you can't find my relatives, be sure to find her a good home."

His chest hurt. "I will."

"She needs someone who can love her."

"Anyone would love the pipsqueak."

The beat of the heart monitor accelerated. "Whatever happens, don't let Burian take her. Use the documents in my quarters, the ones the CIA gave me. They should carry weight in court."

"Eva—"

"Just promise me you'll look out for my daughter. Please, Jack."

"I promise, Eva. I'll make sure Katya gets everything she needs. And Burian will never touch her, I swear."

Dr. Arguin clamped his hand on Jack's shoulder. "You have to leave."

He had a flash of panic. He didn't want to let go of her. He couldn't make himself move until Eva pushed at his chest. Somehow he managed to drop his arms and slide off the bed, then backed through the plastic curtains and left the room. Ten feet down the corridor, his lungs stopped working. He leaned over, braced his hands on his knees and fought for breath.

Damn, this wasn't fair.

But life wasn't fair. He'd already learned that. There were other lessons he'd learned, too. A man had to look out for himself. No strings meant no pain. It was better to be the one doing the leaving than the one who was left. That's why Jack never made promises. People got hurt when they were broken.

So he'd made sure never to linger. He'd convinced himself he wouldn't make a good husband or father. He'd believed he was protecting the women he dated, but in fact he was only protecting himself.

Sex and a good time. A brief time. That's all he'd been willing to share.

Then why was this different? Why had he been willing

to promise Eva anything? Because she wouldn't live long enough to realize when he broke his word?

Jack straightened and drove his fist into the wall. The steel didn't give. He looked at the blood that oozed from his knuckles, welcoming the physical pain. She shouldn't have asked him to look out for Katya. It was an impossible task. He wouldn't be able to find anyone who would be good enough for her. No one would be able to love that child as much as Eva did.

And she was right. The baby needed love. She needed it as much as warmth and food. Otherwise, she would learn how to wall off her heart. How to grow up alone. How to make her career her life and convince herself that her work was all she needed the way Eva had, the way Jack had. And then just when she found someone who made her question all the lessons she'd learned, she would lose them anyway....

His vision blurred. He hit the wall again. He was drawing his arm back for a third blow when someone seized his elbow and spun him around.

"I wouldn't do that, Jack. The wall always wins."

Jack wiped his free hand across his face and saw that Tyler was standing in front of him. Duncan and Kurt were striding toward them, with Gonzo a few steps behind.

"How's she doing?" Duncan asked.

Tyler turned Jack's arm to show them his bleeding knuckles, then released his grip. "Does that answer your question?"

"We heard the diagnosis," Kurt said. "Sorry, man."

Jack folded his arms over his chest. "Yeah."

"At least Ryazan's bug isn't catching."

"Lucky us. If you were coming to see Eva, she's busy with the doctor."

"We were looking for you," Tyler said.

"Why?"

"We're meeting the major. Figured you'd want to come along."

"I'm not going anywhere, junior," Jack said.

Kurt glanced at the other men. "Jack hasn't heard."

"I know the quarantine's been lifted. I'm staying here until Eva…" He inhaled hard through his nose. "She shouldn't be alone. I'll put in for emergency leave."

"You need to know what Tim Shires learned from the CIA's pet scientists," Duncan said.

"What's more to know? They confirmed Eva's got the virus and we don't."

"Sure, but there was stuff on that disk she didn't know about."

He was having a hard time following the conversation. He didn't want to talk. He still wanted to hit something. He turned his wrist to press his knuckles into his sleeve. "It was a big project. Eva worked on only one part. So what?"

"From what Shires said, someone at Ryazan's complex was working on a vaccine."

Overhead, one of the catapults thudded back into action. Jack's pulse took a sudden leap along with it. "There's a vaccine? The virus can be stopped?"

"It looks like it."

Jack lunged forward and grabbed the front of Duncan's shirt. "Why the hell aren't they giving it to her? The doctor never said anything." He let go of Duncan and turned. "They're wasting time. If they can't do it here they should fly her out."

Tyler stepped into his path before he could go past. "It's not that simple, Jack."

"Duncan just said—"

"There's a vaccine," Duncan said. "But the data on Eva's disk was incomplete. That's why they can't use it. Given enough time, they'll probably be able to duplicate the research, but—"

"But Eva doesn't have time."

Kurt nodded. "That's why we're meeting Redinger. The disk doesn't have what she needs, so we're volunteering to go back to the source."

Jack looked from one man to another. They each wore identical, grim expressions. His brain finally kicked into gear. "The source," he said. "You mean the complex."

"It's our bet that Ryazan's either got the vaccine or he has the formula on one of his computers."

"The spooks and their scientists gave it their best shot," Tyler said. "Now it's our turn."

Chapter 11

The floor shook beneath Jack's boots as he paced across the briefing room. Jets were being launched every few minutes to make up for the lockdown of the day before. For more than two days he hadn't wanted to leave the ship, but this morning he couldn't go soon enough. It was already dawn. They'd approached the major more than six hours ago. Every minute they delayed was one less minute that Eva had.

"Cut it out, Jack," Kurt muttered. "You're making me dizzy."

Tyler leaned a shoulder against the wall. "Wonder what's taking Redinger so long."

"He's probably having trouble getting the brass out of bed," Duncan said. "It's still the middle of the night in Washington."

Jack kicked a chair out of his way and started for another circuit of the room.

"We won't be going in until dark anyway," Gonzo said. He folded his arms on the table and lowered his head. "Might as well catch some sleep while we can."

The door to the briefing room opened. Gonzales shot to his feet as Mitchell Redinger strode to the front of the room. Jack and the rest of the team came to attention.

"I'd like to commend you all for your initiative," Redinger said.

Jack tensed. This didn't sound like the start of a mission briefing.

The major's next words proved him right. "However, the Pentagon won't authorize a second incursion into Russian territory."

Only years of discipline kept Jack motionless. He had less success keeping silent. "Sir, it's not really a second mission. Our initial mission isn't over."

"According to my superiors, it is. You accomplished your objective. The CIA is continuing to analyze the data Dr. Petrova provided, and they are confident they have more than enough to make a credible case to the U.N. The Chameleon Virus program will be stopped."

"But the data wasn't complete, Major."

"It's been deemed sufficient for their purpose. The diplomats have already scheduled talks. They don't want to risk provoking the Russians further by sending the team back in."

Jack tightened his hands into fists. He knew what the major meant. All along, the government had considered the information Eva could provide to be more important than she was. The team had suspected as much. So had Eva. That's why she'd been so adamant about concealing that disk.

She wasn't going to get any satisfaction to learn she'd been right.

"Sir, Dr. Petrova risked her life to stop the work on the Chameleon Virus. She didn't have to come forward. The government owes her. So does the rest of the world."

"I used all those arguments and more, Sergeant Norton. The answer was the same."

"Right. Because the pencil-pushing bureaucrats in Washington decided Eva was expendable."

Tyler moved beside Jack and gave him a hard nudge. "Easy, Jack," he muttered.

Jack knew he was skirting the edge of insubordination already, but he didn't care. He stepped forward. "Major Redinger, since the brass won't send the team back into Russia, I volunteer to go on my own."

Redinger's gaze bored into Jack's. "This meeting is over. You men are dismissed. Except for you, Norton."

Tyler gave him another warning nudge before he left. From the corner of his eye Jack could see Duncan frown and shake his head. He knew they were trying to caution him. He'd done the same for other teammates in the past when they had questioned the major's orders. It had no effect. The moment the door closed behind them, he was determined to state his case. "Permission to speak freely, Major?"

"Go ahead."

"I realize one life doesn't mean much to the guys who drive the desks, but I can't stand by and watch Eva die when I know there's a vaccine out there that can help her. I don't give a damn about politics. My only concern is her survival."

"That's become obvious to everyone on this ship. It's a mistake to get personally involved when you're on a mission, and this is why. You lose your objectivity."

"It's true. I have. Eva is my priority now. I can't give up on her. As long as there's hope, I'm going to do everything in my power to see that she lives. If you were in my position, I believe you'd do the same."

Redinger's jaw twitched. He rubbed his thumb over his wedding ring.

Jack had a flash of guilt. He hadn't intended to remind the major of his late wife, but he wasn't going to apologize. If it would help Eva, he'd do whatever it took.

"I'm not without compassion, Norton. I know how difficult it is to accept the loss of a woman you care about. But the army isn't here for our personal convenience. We all have orders to follow."

"Then I'd like to request a leave, sir."

"If you're contemplating going after that vaccine on your own, you'll be acting without permission."

"I understand, Major."

"Have you considered the possible consequences? Without military resources, it could be suicide. Even if you managed to get into the complex and get back in one piece, you could face a court martial. It could end your career. You're a good soldier, Norton. I wouldn't want to see that happen."

Neither would Jack. He loved what he did. It gave him purpose. The army had been the focus of his life for seventeen years. It was his home just like Eagle Squadron was his family.

Yet there was more to life than his work and his duty. His teammates would still be his brothers, whether he saw them every day or not.

But he couldn't imagine not seeing Eva again.

"I'm willing to take the gamble, Major. The way I look at it, I have more to lose if I stay than if I go."

Redinger regarded him in silence for a minute. Jack took his scrutiny without flinching. He knew the major could have him locked in the ship's brig for his honesty, but if that happened, Jack was confident he would find a way out. If he was forced to return to the States, he would find a way back. He wasn't going to let Eva go without a fight.

"Let's get one thing straight, Norton," the major said. "I don't condone your involvement with Dr. Petrova. In fact, it's the last thing I expected from you."

"It surprised the hell out of me, too, sir."

Redinger grunted. "That said, I don't like the decision to disapprove the return mission any more than you do. It's shortsighted. Allowing a high-profile defector to die sends the wrong message to others who may want to cooperate with our government. We're honor-bound to do everything we can to protect the people who ally themselves with us. Unfortunately, in this case, my hands are tied. Officially, I can't help you."

"All I'm asking for is a leave, Major."

"*Officially,* I can't help you," he repeated. "Neither can the current members of Eagle Squadron, or they might be subject to the same disciplinary action as you. It's bad enough I could lose one man over this affair. I don't want to lose the entire team."

"No, sir."

"But without the proper authorization, you won't be able to access military transport, equipment or intelligence, which would mean almost certain failure." He waited. "On the other hand, a private security contractor who has experience with clandestine operations might be able to provide an individual with the kind of resources he would need, without going through official channels. I've heard that Rafe Marek's company has been doing some work in the Middle East. Do you keep in touch with your former teammate?"

"Yes, sir. I do."

"Give him my regards the next time you see him." Redinger glanced at his watch. "I'm granting you a forty-eight hour compassionate leave. How you choose to spend it is up to you. In fact, neither I nor the team will have any knowledge of your actions. You're dismissed, Sergeant."

Jack felt as if he'd been shoving at a door that had suddenly been yanked open. He grinned as he snapped into a salute. "Yes, sir. Thank you, sir!"

Redinger returned the salute but not the smile. "If you're caught, you're done, Norton. The best way to show your gratitude is to make sure that doesn't happen."

"That's a good girl, kitten," Eva said, touching Katya's cheek before she put the empty bottle on the tray table. "You must have been hungry."

Katya bumped her face against the side of Eva's breast.

"Yes, I know it's not the same, but you'd have to switch to a bottle eventually." She shifted the baby to her shoulder and rubbed her back. "Because you're going to get teeth. Little tiny ones in your lower jaw first. That's what the books say. They might hurt when they come through your gums. But don't be scared. It's all part of growing up. You'll need those teeth so you can chew. You'll discover so many wonderful tastes like peaches and bananas. And apples, too. You'll have to start with purees first to let your tummy get used to them, but later you'll be able to bite and chew and swallow."

Katya squirmed, drew up her knees and let out a long series of burps.

Eva smiled and caught Katya's foot. "By next spring, you'll learn these feet are good for more than kicking.

You're going to love being able to move around by yourself. It might hurt when you fall, but I know you'll get right back up. By next winter, you'll be running." She paused, swallowing hard. "I wish I could be there to see your first steps, kitten. I wish I could buy you your first pair of shoes. And bake your first birthday cake. I'd buy you so many dolls and teddy bears and stuffed horses with floppy ears that you'd need an extra room just for your toys."

"She's going to need a baseball glove, too."

She looked up as Jack walked into the room. He'd been back and forth so often during the past day that the medical staff had given up trying to restrict his visits. "Baseball?"

"You don't want to be sexist, do you?" He rounded the bed and squatted in front of the armchair where she sat. "How are you feeling, Eva?"

She tipped her head toward the IV stand that she'd rolled beside the chair. "The medication the doctors are giving me is helping steady my pulse and blood pressure." She didn't mention what the doctors had said about the increasing reduction of her liver function. He likely had noticed the telltale yellow tinge to her skin. "But I think the improvement's due more to the fact they're letting me keep Katya with me."

"They probably wanted some quiet. I heard the fighter pilots were complaining the squirt drowned out the sound of their engines."

She choked on a laugh. "Don't. Whenever you make me smile, I feel like crying more."

He braced his hands on the arms of the chair, leaned around Katya and gave Eva a long kiss.

She closed her eyes, hoping the tears would dry up. They didn't, but that didn't stop her from enjoying the kiss. Seeing Jack was as potent a medicine as seeing her daughter. Like every precious moment with Katya, she didn't know how many more moments she'd have with Jack. She wanted to make the most of every one of them. "Did you come to say good-night?"

He wiped her cheeks with his knuckles. "Not exactly. I've come to say goodbye."

In spite of the medication, her pulse skipped. "You told me this morning that the mission wasn't approved. Have they changed their minds?"

"No. I'm sorry."

It had been Meg Hurlbut who had first broken the news to Eva about the data concerning the vaccine. The CIA agent had been furious over the government's refusal to allow Eagle Squadron back into Russia. Even though Eva had understood—she'd been raised by a diplomat and knew how they thought—it had been devastating to see her earlier suspicions confirmed. Her life wasn't valued as much as her information.

All day Jack had done his best to keep her spirits up. Unlike the rest of her visitors, he didn't dwell on the fact she was dying. He treated her as if she were very much alive. She was fairly certain he'd been the one who had pressured the staff to let her take care of Katya herself. He'd even taken a turn at giving the baby her bottle.

But now he was leaving. She should have realized this would happen. He was a soldier. He had to go where he was told. The army had plenty of other missions. She clutched Katya tighter and willed herself not to break down. "Is the team moving out?"

"Not yet. The other guys are going to be here a while longer. The major volunteered them to do some hand-to-hand combat training with the marines who are on board. To keep them out of trouble. If you need anything while I'm gone, you can ask them or Major Redinger."

"Then where are you going?"

"I've got some personal business to take care of. I should be back in a day or two. I just didn't want to leave without saying goodbye."

She finally noticed what he was wearing. The clean fatigues he'd changed into when they'd arrived on the ship were gone. He was once again dressed in the dark sweater and the pants with all the pockets that he'd worn during the mission. "Where are you going, Jack?"

He smiled. "Just taking a ride with some old friends."

She'd seen that smile before, when he'd spoken about stealing cars or jumping out of moving trucks. "Is it another mission?"

"No, I'm on leave." He rubbed Katya's head. "Be good for your mom, pipsqueak."

"Jack, what's going on?"

Instead of replying, he kissed Eva again. He used his tongue this time. It distracted her, as he'd probably intended. When she opened her eyes once more, he had straightened and stepped back. "I've got to go."

"Wait. If you're not going on a mission, why can't you tell me where you're going?"

"I'll be back as soon as I can."

Something clicked in her mind. She glanced at the scabs on the back of Jack's hand. He'd shown up with split knuckles after he'd heard her diagnosis, yet he hadn't seemed as angry about the decision not to return to the complex as she would have expected. She'd assumed he'd restrained his own reaction because he hadn't wanted to upset her. Now she realized there was another possibility....

"Oh, my God." Holding Katya to her shoulder, Eva used her IV pole for balance and pulled herself to her feet. "I should have known."

"Should you be standing up?"

"You're doing it anyway, aren't you?"

"I don't know what—"

"Of course! You wouldn't have given up. I know you better than that." She rolled the pole forward until she could reach Jack's arm. "You're going back, aren't you!"

"I'm on leave."

"Don't lie to me, Jack. I can see it in your face. You're doing the mission on your own. You're going to get the vaccine."

"Calm down, Eva. You shouldn't—"

"Are you crazy? You'd be disobeying orders. Without the team to help you, you could get killed."

He cupped her shoulders. "The last thing I want is for you to worry."

"Then don't patronize me. Tell me the truth. Are you planning on breaking into the complex? Without backup? Without approval?"

"Eva—"

"Because I'm not going to let you do it. Not for me. I know how much your job means to you. I understand what the team means, too. They're your family. Your home. I want you to be happy just like I want Katya to be happy. I won't let you throw away your future because you still feel responsible for me."

"I'm not."

"I know you're a good man. An honorable man. I can't imagine how I would have gotten through the past five days without you, but I can see I've been selfish. I've been hanging on to you and I shouldn't have. We've known all along our relationship is temporary. If I hadn't caught the virus, we would already have said goodbye."

He plucked Katya from her grasp and carried her to the hospital bed that was serving as her crib. He laid her on her back, checked that the rails were solidly in place and then returned and scooped Eva into his arms.

"Jack!"

"Grab the pole," he said, carrying her toward the armchair.

She snagged the IV stand to roll it with her.

He sat on the chair and settled her on his lap. "First of all, I'm not throwing away my future. I'm taking a calculated risk."

"But—"

"I'm not going to be completely on my own, either. Remember those friends of mine I told you about? The two who went freelance when they left the army?"

"You said they gave up their careers. They left the team."

"Right. Rafe's company is flying me in. He and Flynn will be standing by to give me backup if I need it. They might not be on the team anymore, but they're still my brothers."

"It's still too dangerous. I don't want to think of you risking so much."

"I've faced worse odds. I'm good at my job. I've broken into places that are higher security than Burian's complex." He took her hands in his. "Second, I'm not doing this because I feel responsible for you. Get that straight right now. You might look all delicate with your blond hair and those baby-blue eyes, but I've seen you in action. You've got the heart of a warrior, and you deserve to have a fighting chance."

His words moved her more than she'd thought possible.

She'd never considered herself to be brave. Just look at the way she kept falling apart. She turned her head to dry her cheek on his shoulder.

"Most of all," he said, "I want you to have a future. I want your baby to know what an incredible mother she has. And I want you to have the chance to start that new life you talked about. Find a place with apple trees. Read all the scientific journals you want. Bake every one of the squirt's birthday cakes and teach her to ride a bike. Think about that instead of worrying about me."

"I can't, Jack. I don't want you to get in trouble or to get hurt because of me. I wouldn't be able to live with myself—" She broke off, realizing how absurd that sounded. She wouldn't have to live with herself. If Jack failed, she would die.

Part of her wanted to continue to argue, to keep him safe, to make sure he didn't ruin the career that he loved.

But most of her wanted him to go and to succeed. Minutes ago she'd been without hope. Now Jack was offering to give her a chance at life and, by God, she wanted to grab it. If she hadn't already fallen in love with him, this would have done it for sure.

She loved him?

Of course she loved him. The realization had been building for days. She'd done her best to reason it away, yet she knew in her heart that what she felt for Jack was far deeper than a physical attraction, and it wasn't showing any signs of wearing off. The bond between them might have begun with adrenaline, but it was strengthening with every passing minute. The danger they'd faced together hadn't changed who they were. Instead, it revealed who they were inside.

She'd loved her daughter from the moment she'd seen

her face. It had taken a little longer than that with Jack, but her feelings for him were just as indisputable. She loved this man to the depth of her soul. She wanted him to be happy.

And she was selfish enough to want to be around to see it. "You're determined to risk this?"

"I told you, it's not that big of a risk."

"All right." She kissed him quickly. "Then I'm coming with you."

He blinked. "You can't."

"I want you to succeed, Jack. To do that, you're going to need someone who knows their way around the complex."

"Duncan's given me his satellite shots and everything that intel had on the place. I already know my way around."

"You don't know the interior layout or the patrol schedule of the guards. You won't be able to access Burian's computer except from his lab, and I know where it is." She slid her hands to his chest. "And if there actually is a supply of the vaccine, you wouldn't know where to look for it or recognize it if you see it unless you can read Russian. You need me, Jack."

"You can coach me."

She shook her head. "There isn't time. Take me with you."

"Eva, you need medication."

"You're a medic. You can give me pills. Or injections. It would be almost the same as that IV drip."

"The physical strain on you could be too much."

"What does it matter? Unless I get that vaccine, I'll die anyway."

He tightened his arms around her, rose to his feet and

then leaned over to put her back on the chair. "I can't expose you to more danger, Eva."

"It can't possibly be worse than what I'm facing now." She levered herself up and wheeled her IV pole to follow him. "I might be weak, but so far I'm still capable of moving around. Check with Dr. Arguin. He'll tell you the same thing. I need to be on my feet as long as I can to help keep my lungs clear."

"You'll slow me down."

"Fumbling around without knowing where you're going will slow you down worse. Admit it, Jack. You need a guide, and you know I can help you."

"What about Katya?"

That stopped her. She turned to the bed. Katya was waving her fists in the air and watching the reflected movement in the bed rails. She was concentrating so hard that her eyes crossed.

Eva was torn between a laugh and a sob. She took one of Katya's hands. If she went with Jack, she might not survive the trip. She would be saying goodbye to her baby sooner than she needed to. These next few days could be all the time she'd get with her child, and she wanted to savor every second.

But if she stayed, Jack might not survive. And she would have no hope of it, either. Dammit, she wanted to see Jack grow old as much as she wanted to see Katya grow up. There really was no other choice. Keeping one hand on her daughter, she reached for Jack's fingers.

The connection was more than physical. Something bright flowed from both Katya and Jack, tingling through Eva's skin and into her bones. It was as if the love she felt for them was reflecting back to her and renewing her strength. "You said you wanted to give me a fighting chance, Jack."

"I do."

"Then prove it."

"Eva…"

"You can't truly expect me to stay here and wait to die. Not when I have so much to live for."

Chapter 12

The rush of cold air took Eva's breath away, slicing through the jumpsuit that flapped against her legs. She pressed her back to Jack's warmth and watched the stars creep past the opening in the side of the plane's fuselage.

"Last chance," he said from behind her. "Give the word, and we'll unbuckle you."

She couldn't twist her head because of her helmet. The wide straps of the harness that held her securely to the front of Jack's body didn't allow her much movement. But he didn't need to see her face to know her answer. He could probably feel her resolve in the tension of her body. "No way!" she said. "I'm coming with you."

"Twenty seconds to the drop, Jack."

Eva turned her attention to the large man who stood opposite the hatch. Starlight gleamed on the side of Rafe Marek's face, revealing a network of deep scars from his cheekbone to his jaw. Though his fair hair was far longer than military regulation would dictate, his proud bearing left no doubt as to his former profession. He saw her looking at him and tapped her helmet. "We'll see you later."

"Try not to make it too much later," Flynn O'Toole said as he checked the strap of her goggles. Unlike his companion, there were no imperfections in Flynn's face. Even in the shadows his handsomeness was startling. He grinned at Jack. "We've got a pool going."

"Count me in," Jack said. "Twenty says we're out of there by oh-four-hundred."

The light beside the hatch went from red to green. Flynn stepped back and gave them a thumbs-up.

Jack extended his hand to return the gesture, then wrapped his arm in front of Eva's waist, swung her to the edge of the opening and tipped them out of the plane.

He'd warned her what to expect. Both of his friends had, too, as they had helped her fasten the harness. They'd assured her that doing a tandem parachute jump was the fastest and simplest way to get into the complex. It would eliminate the need for a long walk, which could have been problematic in her condition. Also, the security system was geared to detect movement on the ground, not infiltration from the air. As Jack had put it, the only difficult part would be the really big first step.

She'd thought she would be terrified, but she wasn't. Once again, she was trusting this man with her life. She'd seen for herself the array of weapons he'd strapped to his body, so she knew he was prepared for anything. Most of all, though, she was certain he wouldn't have agreed to bring her along unless he'd believed he could keep her safe.

The lights of the complex glowed beneath them,

growing brighter with alarming speed. Jack pulled the rip cord, jerking them both backward. The noise of the wind eased as the black parachute billowed open. Eva clutched the straps of her harness, doing her best to remain motionless so she didn't interfere while Jack worked the lines on the chute. They drifted in silence, invisible against the darkness, until their descent took them past the perimeter fence. Jack tugged on the lines, expertly spiraling them toward the square structure near the center. Within seconds they were over the roof of the building that housed the laboratories.

Jack flexed his legs and ran a few steps along the roof to dispel the momentum from their landing. While he stowed the parachute and their jumping gear at the base of a ventilation shaft, she took a few moments to get her bearings. Off to her left was the garage where the complex's fleet of armored SUVs were stored. Jack planned to steal one and disable the rest when they were ready to leave. It was another simple plan, but its success depended on them remaining undetected.

Eva continued to look around. Was it only the different vantage point that made the complex look smaller? The long apartment building where she'd moved after Katya was born seemed squat and ugly. The sloping lines of the library were more graceful, but the pale brick it was constructed of appeared bleak. It was the same with the building that held her office. Though light shone from a handful of the windows, it seemed devoid of life. Round streetlamps glowed along the empty sidewalks and lanes. The lawns were yellowed and dead, the flower beds slashes of dark earth.

She'd once thought it looked like a university campus. That could have been wishful thinking so that she would feel at home here. The only truly good memory she had of this place was Katya's birth. She put one hand on her chest, feeling her daughter's absence more strongly than ever. But the baby was fine, she reminded herself. The medical staff on the carrier knew how to take care of her. The rest of Eagle Squadron had promised to look out for her, too.

"Does it hurt?" Jack asked softly.

"No, I'm okay."

"I meant seeing the place again. You never thought you'd be back."

"It seems different. Or maybe I'm different. It's hard to believe it's been less than a week."

"It's been a busy week."

Her chin trembled. "That's one way to put it."

"But I don't think you're different. I think maybe all the stuff that's happened just let you find out more about yourself." He touched his fingertip to her chin. "That's the thing about danger. It helps straighten out priorities."

"Like survival."

"That's why we're here," he said, sliding his fingers to her neck to check her pulse. He took a water bottle from his belt. "Time for your next dose."

With the help of the water, she swallowed the handful of pills he gave her and then leaned on his arm as they went to the access door to the roof. He spent more time disabling the alarm than he needed for opening the lock itself. Once in the stairwell, she followed him down three flights and then directed him through the network of corridors to Burian's private laboratory. Its door had an electronic lock that presented more of a challenge. Eva had used her access card to open it when she'd been here before, but she had left the card behind when she'd fled. Even if she hadn't, she couldn't be sure it would still function. She watched the other doors along the corridor as Jack worked. No light showed from beneath any of them. She wasn't sure what she'd do if someone did show up.

Many of the people who worked here had been her friends. She wouldn't want Jack to hurt them. For all she knew, some of them could have been as ignorant of the Chameleon program as she had been.

The lock finally clicked. Jack motioned for her to stay back as he swung the door open. He pulled a silenced pistol from the holster that was strapped to his thigh, activated the lamp on the headband he wore and stepped inside.

The narrow beam illuminated a long workbench stacked with a skeletal forest of glassware. Jack advanced methodically, directing the light around the room as he checked behind the bench. Storage cupboards for chemicals and equipment stood against the far wall beside a fume hood and a glass-fronted, refrigerated cabinet. In one corner sat the same massive oak desk that had once been in Burian's office at Moscow University. Jack beckoned Eva to come in.

She closed the laboratory door behind her. Her heart was beating harder now than it had during the parachute jump. Like the complex, Burian's lab also looked different from the last time she'd seen it. Maybe it was the darkness that made it seem so sinister. Or the glint of glass from the shadows.

Jack pointed to the computer that sat on a console beside the desk. "If you fire up that thing, I'll check the cold storage."

"Be careful," she reminded him. She switched on the desk lamp and tilted it low so the illumination wouldn't be seen beneath the door. "This office is where I could have been infected."

He laid his gun on top of the refrigerated cabinet and pulled a pair of latex gloves from one of his pockets, along with the paper where she'd written Russian words for him to look for. As Jack sprang the cabinet lock, Eva sat in front of Burian's computer. She tried to ignore the enormity of what they were doing. And the stakes. The last time she'd been here, she'd been looking for information that would guarantee a new life. Now she simply wanted to live.

She fought to keep her fingers steady as she typed commands into the keyboard. A list of files from the Chameleon program filled the screen. She scrolled through them, trying to find what she might have missed the last time. Given Burian's desire for control, any detail pertaining to the project should be here. For the same reason, if a vaccine had been produced, Burian would want to keep a sample in this lab, just as he kept all the drugs that had been produced at the complex. The difficult part would be identifying it.

Glass bottles chinked as Jack pushed the top tray back into the cabinet and slid out the next one. "Most of the smaller ones only have numbers."

"They could be dates."

"Okay, that fits. Which ones should I look for?"

She concentrated on the names of the files on the screen. "Look for something within the last month. The research has to be recent. Otherwise, there would have been more information…" She stopped and tilted her head toward the door. Had she heard a scraping noise in the corridor? The guards weren't due to make their rounds for another thirty minutes at least.

"You'd better get down, Eva," Jack whispered, retrieving his gun.

The noise hadn't been her imagination. Her pulse continued to accelerate. She gulped in a few deep breaths; then she grabbed the edge of the desk and slid from the chair to the floor.

He motioned for her to switch off the lamp as he crossed the room. He placed himself behind the door just as it swung open.

A man's form was silhouetted in the doorway briefly before the overhead lights blinked on. White hair gleamed in the sudden illumination.

Eva put her hand over her mouth to keep from crying out. Burian. Oh, God. What was he doing here? Why now? He was an early riser. She'd never known him to work after midnight.

Oddly, he appeared as if he were going to attend a meeting rather than work in the lab. His hair was neatly combed, and his cheeks were gleaming from a fresh shave. The camel overcoat he wore was unbuttoned, revealing a dark gray suit and a crisp white shirt accented by his trademark royal blue tie. Holding a briefcase under his arm, he swung the door shut behind him.

Before he'd gone three steps, Jack moved behind him, fisted one hand in the back of his collar and pressed the muzzle of his gun beneath Burian's ear. "That's far enough, Dr. Ryazan."

Burian froze. His expression went blank with shock. Within seconds the shock gave way to anger. "You are making a grave mistake." He spoke English with slow precision, his accent adding an edge to his words. "Release me immediately."

"I can't do that." Maintaining the pressure with his gun, Jack reached around to take the briefcase, dropped it to the floor and then patted the sides of Burian's coat. He withdrew a cell phone, tossed it beside the briefcase and reached into his own pocket to withdraw a thin plastic strap. "Put your hands behind your back."

"If you do not release me, you will not leave here alive."

"For a smart guy," Jack remarked, "that's a dumb threat. I'm the one holding the gun."

In movements that were too quick for Eva to follow, Jack jerked Burian's arms back and fastened the plastic around his wrists. The strap was a bundling tie, she realized. Moments later, Jack had Burian sitting on the floor and had fastened another plastic tie around his ankles.

Burian strained against his bonds. He toppled sideways, his fall halted when he struck his shoulder on the side of the workbench. He used his elbow to push himself upright again and glared at Jack. "Who are you? What do you want?"

Eva felt a twinge of pity. For a man who was accustomed to being in control, it would be humiliating to be physically humbled. She used the desk to pull herself to her feet. "He's with me, Burian."

He whipped his head around. A smile lit his face. "Eva! How did you..." His smile faded as he looked from her to Jack. "I see. So it was the Americans who helped you leave me. Who is this thug?"

"He is my friend."

Burian raked Jack with a dismissive glance. "He has the look of a common soldier. He could not possibly be your friend."

Jack snorted at the insult. "Is he always this annoying, Eva?"

"Where is my daughter?" Burian demanded.

"She's safe."

"You will bring her to me."

Jack shook his head. "You're not going to get anywhere near that kid. But as long as you're here, you might as well make yourself useful and save everyone some time."

Burian surveyed the room, looking from the open cabinet to the humming computer. His expression smoothed. "Of course. That is why you came back, Eva. I had expected to hear from you when you understood what I had done, but I had not anticipated a move as bold as this."

His lack of surprise unnerved her. "What you had done?" Eva repeated.

"It was intended as a lesson. I had not wanted to harm you, but you needed to learn that you could not continue to defy me."

"Burian, what—"

"This would not have happened if you had stayed where you belonged," he continued. "Now it may be too late. Your color is not good. It is clear the Chameleon Virus has progressed past its first stages."

It sounded as if Burian guessed that she was infected. But how could that be? The doctors had confirmed her diagnosis only a day ago. And what kind of lesson...

Understanding flashed through her brain. She rounded the desk, her body shaking with fury. And she had been on the verge of feeling sorry for him? "You bastard."

"As usual, your emotions are clouding your logic, Eva. Have I not taught you better? This is your doing. If you had not left me, we would have reached a new understanding by now."

Jack leaned over to grab the front of Burian's overcoat. "What the hell are you talking about?"

"Explain it to your thug, Eva. He does not appear capable of higher reasoning."

"Your insults are pointless, Burian. He's a better man than you could ever hope to be. Next to him, I wouldn't even call you a man." Eva could feel the room spinning. She braced her hand on the workbench and tried to rein in her anger. She looked at Jack. "I was wrong. I wasn't infected accidentally."

"Did you believe you were?" Burian asked. "That disappoints me, Eva. You know that the Chameleon Virus is too stable to present any danger unless it is activated. It cannot be contracted by mistake."

Jack hauled Burian to his feet. "Are you saying you *deliberately* infected her?"

"There is no other way. That is one of the beauties of my creation. It is only activated in liquids. It can target one individual or an entire population."

Burian spoke as if he were proud, and he likely was. Eva inhaled hard, trying to catch her breath. "How, Burian?"

"Our last staff meeting, of course. I put it in your tea."

That was two days before she'd left. So she already had the virus before she'd come to this lab. And she had two days less to live than she'd thought she had. "Damn you, Burian. How could you do this to me?"

Burian twisted against Jack's grip as he tried to face Eva. "It was your fault. You left me. You cannot imagine my worry when I went to your quarters only to discover that you had disappeared. I ordered a search immediately. They were to stop you and bring you back." He looked at Jack. "I assume you were among those who aided her. You should not have interfered."

"You wanted to kill me," Eva said.

"No. It should be obvious that I would not have infected you if I could not have reversed it. You were of too much value to me. I was prepared to give you a choice that would allow you to prove your loyalty to me. The day you left should have been a new beginning for our love. Instead, you ruined it."

Her chest hurt from her urge to scream. She had thought Burian only wanted Katya. Yet all along, Jack had refused to believe that. He'd been convinced Burian wouldn't willingly let Eva go.

He'd been right.

"Don't you dare speak about love," Eva said. "You don't understand the meaning of the word. All you know is control and possession. And what kind of choice did you think you were giving me? You mean if I had agreed to renew our affair, you would have let me live?"

"You needed to learn it was the only logical option. We are perfect for each other, Eva. I planned to have you at my side as we changed the course of the world. Now more than ever you needed to understand you belong to me."

Jack tightened his grip on Burian and shook him hard enough to snap his head back. "Okay, now I'm giving you a choice. You said you could reverse what you did to Eva. Do it and I might let you live."

"You will not kill me," he gasped.

"Don't bet on it." Jack half carried, half dragged Burian around the bench to the open door of the refrigerated cabinet. "Which one of these is the vaccine?"

Instead of replying, Burian looked at Eva. "I did not plan to harm you. If you had not left me, you would not be ill."

Jack shook him again. "Look, buddy, you might have a bunch of fancy degrees after your name, and you might have the rest of the world fooled, but you're no different from the other nutbars out there who figure they've got a right to abuse women."

"Preposterous. I am no abuser."

"You abused her trust. You abused her innocence. You—" He broke off. A muscle in his cheek twitched. "This isn't getting us anywhere. Where's the vaccine?"

Burian studied Jack. "You are very passionate about Eva's fate. Why is that? What did she promise you?"

"I have an idea. I'll start injecting you with the stuff that's in these bottles until I find one that cures stupidity."

"What do you value? What is your price?"

Jack shoved Burian down to sit on the floor, holstered his gun and lifted a tray of glass vials from the cabinet. He set it on the workbench, then took his trimmed-down med kit from a pocket and withdrew a syringe. "How much time do we have before the guards do their next rounds, Eva?"

She wasn't sure whether or not Jack was bluffing. Judging by the look on his face, he could easily do murder. He opened a vial at random, inserted the tip of the syringe and drew back the plunger. He repeated the process with five more vials until the syringe was filled to its capacity with a cloudy, yellow mixture.

God help her, but she didn't *want* this to be a bluff. She wanted Burian to suffer, to learn the helplessness that she was feeling, to know fear. He'd stolen her life and her future. She felt no pity for him. "Fifteen minutes," she said.

"That should give us plenty of time to see how he reacts to this brew."

Burian used his feet to push himself along the floor on his rear. "This is barbaric."

Jack hooked Burian's bound ankles with the toe of one boot to stop his retreat. "What do you expect? I'm a thug, remember? Just tell me where the vaccine is. Or is your desire to punish Eva worth more to you than your life?"

"My guards will kill you."

"They can try. They didn't do that good a job before, did they?" He squatted beside Burian and poised the needle over his thigh. "I wonder what's in this stuff. Hey, do you keep samples of the Chameleon Virus in that cabinet, too?"

Burian's eyes flicked to the tray of vials. It was evident by his dawning expression of horror that Jack's guess was correct. "Eva, stop him!"

With the thought of Katya growing up motherless and Jack growing old alone, she pressed her lips together and said nothing.

"Maybe you'll be lucky." Jack depressed the plunger, forcing out a few drops of liquid from the tip. They produced a dark circle on Burian's pantleg. "Then again, maybe not. Are you a gambling man, Dr. Ryazan?"

"Bring me my daughter, and you can have the vaccine."

Jack halted. "What?"

"It is Eva you want, is it not? That is why you are so emotional."

"You're not in a position to make bargains."

"On the contrary. I am prepared to give you what you ask. I will provide the vaccine, you can have the woman, but only when I have the child."

Jack's fingers cramped on the syringe. It took every scrap of willpower he possessed to keep his arm motionless. He didn't want to use the needle on Burian. He wanted to use his fist.

How could anyone, even a demented bastard like this one, think of separating Eva from her baby? It would be the same as asking her to cut off an arm. Or cut out her heart. A woman like Eva would fight to the death to protect the child she loved. Jack understood that. He'd seen it for himself. It was how he felt about them both.

Eva stumbled into the workbench, knocking over a pair of empty beakers that were clamped to a metal stand. Glass shattered on the floor.

Jack got to her side just as her knees gave. She clutched his arms and leaned toward Burian. "No!" she cried. "You're not getting Katya!"

"I am her father, Eva."

"You don't love her."

He lifted his shoulders. It was an arrogant gesture for a man who was bound hand and foot. He appeared to be empowered by the effect he was having on Eva. "She is merely an infant. Love is immaterial. It is guidance that she needs, not sentiment. I will teach my daughter to be strong, like me."

Eva's cheeks had paled. She was fighting for breath. "Jack…"

He picked her up and carried her to the chair behind the desk. Once she was seated, he gave her another dose of the medications Dr. Arguin had prepared. "Try to stay calm, Eva," he said, holding his water bottle to her lips. "Your pulse rate is too high."

"You can't help her," Burian said. "The symptoms will continue to worsen. Without my help, in another five days, her liver will fail. Fluid will gather around her internal organs. Her heart will not endure the strain. You have no time to waste. Where is the child? I will send my people for her."

Jack squeezed Eva's hands and looked at Burian. "You're not getting anywhere near that baby. You're not fit to raise a lab rat."

"What bluster. You are the one who is annoying. I have more friends and resources than you can imagine. If you do not accept my bargain…" He looked toward the door. His lips stretched into a smile. "I believe our negotiations are finished. My men are early."

There was the stamp of boots outside. Someone was shouting orders in the corridor.

Had their parachute gear been found? Jack looked at Eva. She was in no shape to make a run for the stairs. And if he carried her, he wouldn't be able to fire with any accuracy.

But leaving without the vaccine wasn't an option, anyway.

He dragged the desk across the room to barricade the door. Seconds later, it reverberated with a heavy knock. A male voice came through the steel panel, calling out something in Russian. The only words Jack understood were Burian's name.

"You should have accepted my offer," Burian said. "Now you both will die."

Jack wedged the desk firmly against the door. The heavy oak should buy them some time. After that…

He returned to Eva and knelt beside her chair. "Get everything you can off that computer," he said. "The formula has to be in there. We'll find someone to duplicate the vaccine when we get out of here."

She was too smart to buy into his attempt to cheer her. Instead of reaching for the keyboard, she touched his face. It was clear by the sadness in her eyes that she understood there was little hope of escape. "I'm sorry, Jack. I should have stopped you from coming. I knew it was too risky."

"You couldn't have stopped me, Eva. I would have tried anyway."

The door shook from the impact of a heavy object. Plaster dust wafted down from the ceiling. Burian managed to get his legs under him and rose to his knees, shouting encouragement.

Eva trembled. She traced the lines beside Jack's mouth and then touched both hands to the corners of his eyes. "I wish we had met sooner."

"So do I." He turned his head to kiss her palm. "But then we would have missed all this fun."

A tear crept down her cheek. "That's right. You sure know how to show a girl a good time."

His own eyes filled with moisture. He hadn't cried since he'd been fourteen and standing beside his mother's grave. It was the last time he'd allowed himself to love anyone.

The next blow on the door opened a split in the door frame. Jack could see the lights in the corridor. It was only a matter of seconds before the guards would break through.

Jack wanted more than a few more seconds with Eva. He didn't want to measure their time in mere days. He wanted to sleep with her every night and wake up with her every morning, feel her hair slide between his fingers, hear her laugh, watch her eat and let her steal the bread from his plate. He wanted the chance to see her play with her baby again—and see her stomach grow round with another one. He wanted to be there to teach Katya how to ride a bike or oil a baseball glove or even tie ribbons in her doll's hair if that's what she asked. All the ordinary, everyday things a family did...

Damn.

He cupped the back of Eva's head and kissed her with all the pent-up frustration he felt. Now that he'd found a woman he could see in his future, chances were they wouldn't have one.

The door gave with a crash, crushing the desk into splinters. Jack broke off the kiss and placed himself in front of Eva.

The first man who came through didn't look like one of guards from the complex. He wore the uniform of a Russian soldier. Four more soldiers entered behind him. They bypassed Jack and Eva and converged on Burian, their weapons drawn. One man yanked him to his feet while another shouted questions.

Jack felt behind him for Eva's hand. "What are they saying?"

"Oh, my God," she breathed. "I don't believe this."

"What?"

"It sounds as if they're arresting him."

Chapter 13

Katya was running between the trees, afternoon sunlight dappling her white-blond pigtails and her arms full of ripe apples. She slid to a stop beside the basket, let the fruit tumble and gave Eva a gap-toothed grin. Then she ran to Jack, laughter and a hair ribbon trailing behind her.

He swung her into his arms and lifted her high so she could reach the branches with the ripest apples.

Eva drew the blanket over her shoulders as she walked toward them. The breeze was getting cool. It was almost time to go home, but she didn't feel any urgency. She knew how to get there. She wasn't lost.

Home was where it always had been. It wasn't a place but a feeling.

The sunlight faded. The scent of grass and ripe apples became cotton, bleach and the perfume of flowers. Eva stretched out her hand. "Jack?"

His fingers closed gently around hers. "I'm right here, Eva."

She opened her eyes.

The dream melded with reality. Jack was sitting beside her hospital bed. He was holding Katya to his shoulder with one hand while he clasped Eva's fingers with the other. "How are you doing?" he asked.

She pushed herself up on one elbow. "Better every day."

"I heard you're getting discharged this afternoon."

"That's what the doctors told me."

"Are you still going to that hotel room the spooks got for you?"

"For a while, at least."

"You'll need a moving van for all these flowers."

She let go of his hand and sat up. During the two weeks since she'd arrived in Washington, there had been new arrangements delivered daily. Every available surface in the hospital room was crammed with bouquets and gifts, many from people she hadn't met. There were lilies from an official at the State Department, a potted orchid from the director of the CIA and a silver samovar from the Russian ambassador.

The Russian government was as grateful to Eva as the Americans. It turned out that Burian had deceived them along with everyone else. They had been completely unaware of the Chameleon Virus program until the Americans had scheduled talks in order to stop it. Burian hadn't meant to give his weapon to his own country. In his twisted view of fairness, he had planned to sell it to the highest bidder.

The Russian raid on the complex had almost been too late. Burian had been scheduled to meet with a buyer that very night. It was why he had gone to his laboratory—he'd meant to pick up samples of both the virus and the vaccine to take with him. It was also why he'd infected Eva the week before—he'd imagined that would have given him enough time to convince her to share his triumph. In his mind, he believed himself justified in everything he'd done.

If Burian hadn't been delayed by Jack and Eva, he might have gotten away with it.

It had taken less than an hour for the Russians to provide her with the vaccine that saved her life. She'd never asked how they had persuaded Burian to part with the information. Some things were better left alone. Eva still got chills whenever she thought of how easily the outcome could have been different.

She pulled up her feet beneath the blanket and wrapped her arms around her legs. Then she rested her cheek on her knees as she regarded Jack. He was wearing his dress uniform today. Katya appeared fascinated with the ribbons on his chest. Eva could understand that. In that uniform, Jack looked good enough to stare at all day….

She lifted her head quickly. "The hearing," she said. "It was supposed to be this morning, wasn't it?"

He nodded.

"What happened?"

"I was given an official reprimand for assaulting a foreign civilian during my leave."

"That's all?"

He grinned. "The major called in some favors. The Russians did, too. Turns out the guys who did the raid were from their Special Forces. They were pretty impressed by how we got there before them and wanted to show me some professional courtesy."

"Jack, that's wonderful! Then you're still with Eagle Squadron."

"Oh, yeah. They're stuck with me."

"I'm so glad. I know how much it means to you."

He stood, carried Katya to the bassinet at the foot of the bed and laid her on her back. She gurgled, batting at the plastic beads he'd strung across it the day before. He ruffled Katya's hair and gave the beads a spin before he returned to Eva's side. "Belonging to Eagle Squadron does mean a lot to me," he said. "My work has been the most important thing in my life."

"I understand."

"But I have to come clean, Eva. I haven't been completely honest with you."

He was smiling, so she didn't think he was going to say something that would upset her. Still, since they'd returned to the States and reality had set in, they hadn't spoken of much except her health, the mission and its aftermath. She had wanted to wait until she was well again before she pushed him about their relationship. She knew how seriously he took his honor. She didn't want him staying with her out of duty or pity.

There was no longer any time limit on her future. She was going to recover. She had all the time in the world to make Jack love her.

"Rafe and Flynn send their regards," he said. "They were at the hearing today."

"They're good men. I owe them a lot."

"You don't owe them anything. They're family. It evens out." He took her hand. "But there's something else you need to know about them. I told you they'd each gone through the same kind of adrenaline attraction during a mission that you and I did."

Some of her confidence ebbed. "Yes, I remember. It's why they left the army."

"Not exactly. In Rafe's case, the attraction wasn't temporary. He ended up marrying a hostage he rescued. That was seven years ago. His wife's the one who financed his new company."

"What?"

"She comes from old money. She also owns a few hotels. Flynn got involved with a civilian during another mission. That wasn't temporary, either. He and Abbie celebrated their fifth anniversary last month. They're expecting twins next year."

"Oh."

"And I told you about Sarah, our former intelligence specialist."

"You said she quit the team to have children."

"The father of her children is the man she'd once been assigned to guard." He twined his fingers with hers. "I didn't tell you this before because I was scared, Eva. I'd been on my own for so long that I didn't want to change. But these past few weeks haven't really changed me. They just showed me what I truly wanted. Not all the feelings that get stirred up during a mission wear off."

Her heart began to pound. The virus was gone from her body, so she knew the cause wasn't physical. "No, they don't. Some of them are too deep to wear off."

"I know I don't have a great track record when it comes to relationships. I don't know anything about babies or raising kids. The missions I'll be going on will take me away for days at a stretch, sometimes weeks. I can't understand the kind of work that you do. Hell, I can't even do my own taxes. I watch too much football, I can't cook and if I have a few beers I end up snoring all night."

She laid her hand against his jaw. "You won't be able to talk me out of loving you, Jack, no matter how hard you try."

"I'm not trying to talk you out of..." He paused. "What did you say?"

"I love you, Jack."

He closed his eyes and pressed his lips to her hand. He breathed deeply a few times, as if he'd just run a race. "Damn, and I had a great speech planned."

She laughed. "Go ahead. I won't stop you."

"Okay. I don't want you and Katya to go to a hotel when you leave here. I want you to come back to Bragg with me. Live with me. Marry me. Let me be a father to your baby. Give her a whole houseful of toys and sisters and brothers to play with."

"Sisters and brothers?"

He picked up the chair, carried it to the door and angled it beneath the handle to hold it shut. Peeling off his jacket, he returned to the bed.

"Jack? What are you doing?"

"The docs said you're recovered. You can resume your normal activities." He toed off his shoes, got on the bed and pulled her into his arms. "I've been waiting for weeks to tell you I love you. I think it would be better to show you instead."

Eva smiled as she sank into Jack's kiss.

And she knew she was finally home.

* * * * *

*Coming in June 2010 from Silhouette Romantic
Suspense Books…Ingrid Weaver's thrilling new
Eagle Squadron: Countdown story,*
ACCIDENTAL COMMANDO!
Read on for an exciting sneak peek!

Something scraped outside her door. The lock clicked
and it swung open to the limit of the chain. Emily
watched, horrified, as the door kept moving. The bracket
that held the chain slowly pulled out of the wall. A tall,
blond man stepped over the threshold and nudged the
door closed with his boot heel.

This was the man who had tackled her, all right.
Those were the same worn, black, cowboy boots she'd
seen beside her nose. A pair of jeans draped his long
legs, a pale yellow golf shirt stretched across his broad
shoulders and ropy muscles contoured his arms. His
body looked just the way it had felt. Big, solid, and very
male. The only thing she hadn't been able to feel when
he'd pinned her to the floor was the rifle that was slung
over his back.

Finally, Emily did scream. She dropped the receiver
and ran for the bathroom.

The blond man caught her from behind before she'd
gone two steps. He slid one arm in front of her waist,
lifted her from her feet and backed up so he could hang
up the phone. Then he clamped his free hand over her
mouth. "I'm not going to hurt you, but I can't let you call
the police."

Harlequin Intrigue top author
Delores Fossen presents
a brand-new series of breathtaking
romantic suspense!
TEXAS MATERNITY: HOSTAGES
The first installment available May 2010:
THE BABY'S GUARDIAN

Shaw cursed and hooked his arm around Sabrina.

Despite the urgency that the deadly gunfire created, he tried to be careful with her, and he took the brunt of the fall when he pulled her to the ground. His shoulder hit hard, but he held on tight to his gun so that it wouldn't be jarred from his hand.

Shaw didn't stop there. He crawled over Sabrina, sheltering her pregnant belly with his body, and he came up ready to return fire.

This was obviously a situation he'd wanted to avoid at all cost. He didn't want his baby in the middle of a fight with these armed fugitives, but when they fired that shot, they'd left him no choice. Now, the trick was to get Sabrina safely out of there.

"Get down," someone on the SWAT team yelled from the roof of the adjacent building.

Shaw did. He dropped lower, covering Sabrina as best he could.

There was another shot, but this one came from a rifleman on the SWAT team. Shaw didn't look up, but he heard the sound of glass being blown apart.

The shots continued, all coming from his men, which meant it might be time to try to get Sabrina to better cover. Shaw glanced at the front of the building.

So that Sabrina's pregnant belly wouldn't be smashed

against the ground, Shaw eased off her and moved her to a sitting position so that her back was against the brick wall. They were close. Too close. And face-to-face.

He found himself staring right into those sea-green eyes.

How will Shaw get Sabrina out?
Follow the daring rescue and the heartbreaking
aftermath in THE BABY'S GUARDIAN
by Delores Fossen,
available May 2010 from Harlequin Intrigue.

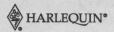

HARLEQUIN®
INTRIGUE®

HARLEQUIN
Ambassadors

Want to share your passion for reading Harlequin® Books?

Become a Harlequin Ambassador!

Harlequin Ambassadors are a group of passionate and well-connected readers who are willing to share their joy of reading Harlequin® books with family and friends.

You'll be sent all the tools you need to spark great conversation, including free books!

All we ask is that you share the romance with your friends and family!

You'll also be invited to have a say in new book ideas and exchange opinions with women just like you!

To see if you qualify* to be a Harlequin Ambassador, please visit
www.HarlequinAmbassadors.com.

*Please note that not everyone who applies to be a Harlequin Ambassador will qualify. For more information please visit www.HarlequinAmbassadors.com.

Thank you for your participation.

BAP09BPA

Bestselling Harlequin Presents® author

Lynne Graham

introduces

VIRGIN ON HER WEDDING NIGHT

Valente Lorenzatto never forgave Caroline Hales's
abandonment of him at the altar. But now he's
made millions and claimed his aristocratic Venetian
birthright—and he's poised to get his revenge.
He'll ruin Caroline's family by buying out their
company and throwing them out of their mansion…
unless she agrees to give him the wedding night
she denied him five years ago.…

**Available May 2010
from Harlequin Presents!**

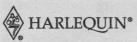

HARLEQUIN®

American ★ Romance®

LAURA MARIE ALTOM

The Baby Twins

Stephanie Olmstead has her hands full raising
her twin baby girls on her own. When she runs
into old friend Brady Flynn, she's shocked to find
herself suddenly attracted to the handsome airline
pilot! Will this flyboy be the perfect daddy—
or will he crash and burn?

Babies
&
Bachelors
USA

"LOVE, HOME & HAPPINESS"

www.eHarlequin.com

HAR75309

REQUEST YOUR FREE BOOKS!

2 FREE NOVELS
PLUS
2 FREE GIFTS!

Silhouette

ROMANTIC
SUSPENSE

Sparked by Danger, Fueled by Passion.

YES! Please send me 2 FREE Silhouette® Romantic Suspense novels and my 2 FREE gifts (gifts are worth about $10). After receiving them, if I don't wish to receive any more books, I can return the shipping statement marked "cancel." If I don't cancel, I will receive 4 brand-new novels every month and be billed just $4.24 per book in the U.S. or $4.99 per book in Canada. That's a saving of 15% off the cover price! It's quite a bargain! Shipping and handling is just 50¢ per book.* I understand that accepting the 2 free books and gifts places me under no obligation to buy anything. I can always return a shipment and cancel at any time. Even if I never buy another book from Silhouette, the two free books and gifts are mine to keep forever.

240/340 SDN E5Q4

Name	(PLEASE PRINT)	
Address		Apt. #
City	State/Prov.	Zip/Postal Code

Signature (if under 18, a parent or guardian must sign)

Mail to the Silhouette Reader Service:
IN U.S.A.: P.O. Box 1867, Buffalo, NY 14240-1867
IN CANADA: P.O. Box 609, Fort Erie, Ontario L2A 5X3

Not valid for current subscribers to Silhouette Romantic Suspense books.

Want to try two free books from another line?
Call 1-800-873-8635 or visit www.morefreebooks.com.

* Terms and prices subject to change without notice. Prices do not include applicable taxes. N.Y. residents add applicable sales tax. Canadian residents will be charged applicable provincial taxes and GST. Offer not valid in Quebec. This offer is limited to one order per household. All orders subject to approval. Credit or debit balances in a customer's account(s) may be offset by any other outstanding balance owed by or to the customer. Please allow 4 to 6 weeks for delivery. Offer available while quantities last.

Your Privacy: Silhouette is committed to protecting your privacy. Our Privacy Policy is available online at www.eHarlequin.com or upon request from the Reader Service. From time to time we make our lists of customers available to reputable third parties who may have a product or service of interest to you. If you would prefer we not share your name and address, please check here. ☐
Help us get it right—We strive for accurate, respectful and relevant communications. To clarify or modify your communication preferences, visit us at www.ReaderService.com/consumerschoice.

SRS10R